The
Reluctant
Tracker

The
Reluctant
Tracker

Robert W. Callis

THE RELUCTANT TRACKER

iUniverse books may be ordered through booksellers or by contacting:

iUniverse
1663 Liberty Drive
Bloomington, IN 47403
www.iuniverse.com
844-349-9409

ISBN: 978-1-6632-4077-4 (sc)
ISBN: 978-1-6632-4078-1 (e)

Library of Congress Control Number: 2022910550

Print information available on the last page.

iUniverse rev. date: 06/01/2022

Dedication

This book is dedicated to my late cousin Tom Main. Tom was the smartest member of my family. He was a rocket scientist. He graduated from Knox College with a bachelor's degree and then was drafted into the United States Army. He served as an officer and spent most of his enlistment stationed in Germany. When Tom finished his enlistment, the army asked him to be an instructor at West Point. He declined the offer, enrolled at Dartmouth, and earned a master's degree. Tom was highly intelligent, but he was also kind and appreciative of others. He was the humblest man I ever knew. He made the world around him a better place.

Chapter One

Kit kept one eye on the electronic map in the dash of his pickup truck. He listened to the electronic voice giving him directions, but he preferred to see where the voice was taking him. The screen was enlarged to do just that.

He had spent the last four days on his latest job, finding a runaway seventeen-year-old girl for her distraught parents. She had run off with a man she had met on the internet and the parents had called Kit after the local sheriff's office had seemed disinterested in their plight. How the parents had found Kit was at first a mystery. They lived in Salt Lake City, Utah, and while he was familiar with Salt Lake City, he had never done any client work there. His only connection to the area was an incident several years before when he left a car with the keys in the ignition and walked away from it for the express purpose of having it stolen and stripped. It was a case where he had done his best to remain invisible and unknown. To the best of his knowledge, he had succeeded.

The parents Bill and Alyssa Bergstrom had gotten a phone call from their daughter Wendy. They had written down the number of the pay phone she had used to trace its location when it appeared on their call system.

Someone had read their plea for help on the internet and directed them to Kit's company Rocky Mountain Searchers

1

located in Kemmerer, Wyoming. They had called Kit and then sent him recent photos and information on their missing daughter and her internet boyfriend Mac Stone.

Kit had been moved by Alyssa, the girl's mother, when she pleaded on the telephone for his help. He had always been a sucker for a woman in distress. Any woman, old or young, had the same effect on him. By the time Bill and Alyssa had contacted Kit, Wendy had been missing for four days. It had taken him less than an hour using the pay phone number for him to locate where Wendy might be.

In this day and age of cell phones, land lines were becoming scarce and pay phones even more scarce. The most likely places to have a pay phone were locations like bars, gas stations, and coin operated laundromats. The latter was where the pay phone Wendy had called her parents was located. A call to his data specialist friend had given him the location of the phone in less than three minutes. He found the pay phone located in a small laundromat in a low-end campground just south of Glacier National Park in Montana.

Kit looked up the campground on the internet and found it listed, but with minimal information. It did mention a laundromat. It was obviously at the bottom of the food chain for laundromats in Montana. In this case, the area around the national park. Kit had driven for about fourteen hours and stopped at a motel in Kalispell, Montana. He had planned to stay the night, then get up early and drive to the campground and stake out the laundromat. The trip was uneventful. The weather was good for early September, and the traffic got lighter the further north he went. The only surprise he got during the trip was when he stopped at a motel to get a room. The surprise was the price. A simple room was three hundred and fifty dollars a night. Kit took it, as he was tired and running out of energy. He left the motel and found a mom-and-pop restaurant about a mile away. The service and the food were both good. He pulled out his phone to check motel rates while he waited for his meal to arrive. He discovered his room was at the low end of cost for anything respectable in Kalispell. Kit chalked it up to tourists coming to Glacier National Park. After finishing his meal, he paid for it, tipped the waitress, and headed back to the motel. Kit was asleep as soon as his head hit the pillow.

His alarm jarred him awake at four-thirty in the morning. He showered, shaved, and got dressed. He found a drive-thru restaurant and grabbed a coffee and breakfast sandwich. When he reached the campground, he quickly found the laundromat. He parked his truck a good distance away, but with an unobstructed view of the entrance. He sat back in his seat and ate his sandwich and sipped his coffee. He placed two recent enlarged photos of Wendy on the dash and accepted his current fate. He waited.

As Kit waited, he carefully studied his surroundings. The campground had small spaces, grouped too close together for his taste. Here and there were large pine and cedar trees, survivors of too many campers, tents, RVs, and a lack of effective trash collection. The nearest trash bin was overflowing, and trash lay scattered on the ground all around the bin. It was obvious man was nature's greatest enemy. Kit knew this campground was one of the least expensive available near the park and thus suffered from overuse and lack of basic care. Grass was almost non-existent, and even weeds were few in number in the hard packed soil.

An hour slipped into two, and Kit began to wonder if he had gotten the wrong campsite from the campground's website. He checked his iPad, but the campsite was the one rented by Mack Stone. He smiled to himself. The dumb bastard was so stupid he didn't even bother to use a fake name when he rented the campsite online.

Kit looked above the campsite, up into the mountains to the west and to the north. They looked enormous, but he knew from his research they were smaller, at least in height, to the Tetons near his home in Wyoming.

The silence of the nearly vacant campground was interrupted by the sound of a loud, but small engine. Sure enough, a Polaris Ranger UTV roared past where he was parked and continued until it passed through the campground and headed east as it kept going. Kit was about to check his watch for the tenth time when he heard the unmistakable sound of loud mufflers on a vehicle with an engine that was running less than smoothly.

Kit sat up in his seat, alert and ready. His hand moved as he unconsciously checked to make sure his pistol was secure in the holster on his hip.

The old Dodge pickup truck pulled into the campground and pulled up next to the ragged tent occupying the campsite. Kit slouched down in his seat and kept his eyes on the two figures who emerged from the old truck. The man was young, skinny, and looked undernourished. He sported a filthy shirt with jeans to match and an old feed store cap. The girl was young, and she matched the photo Kit had on the dash of his pickup. He knew he was looking at Wendy Bergstrom.

Kit waited until the couple unloaded some bags of what looked like food from the truck and deposited them in the old tent. While they were in the tent, Kit slipped out of his truck and quietly closed the door. He slowly approached the tent, careful to not make any unnecessary noise. When he was about ten feet from the tent, he stopped. He put his right hand on the butt of his pistol and spread his feet until they were just under his shoulders. The perfect shooter's stance.

He didn't have to wait long. After a couple of minutes, the young man emerged from the tent and surprise was frozen on his face as he saw Kit for the first time.

"Put your hands behind your head and turn around," commanded Kit.

5

Mack Stone was young, but he wasn't completely stupid. He did as he was told.

"Now get down on your knees," said Kit.

Almost immediately, Wendy appeared outside the tent, shock, and astonishment on her face.

"Are you Wendy Bergstrom?" asked Kit, not taking his eyes off the kneeling Mack.

"Yes, yes I am," Wendy blurted out. "Who are you?"

"I'm the man your parents hired to find you and bring you safely home," replied Kit.

"Oh, thank God," said Wendy as she fell to her knees, crying and sobbing.

Crying women always made Kit feel extremely uncomfortable. He let her cry and waited a few minutes before he spoke.

"Wendy, get your stuff packed," said Kit. "We're leaving."

Wendy stopped sobbing and got to her feet. She retreated into the old tent and soon emerged with a small backpack.

"That's all your stuff?" asked Kit.

"Yes sir," said Wendy. "That's all I have in the world."

Kit nodded his understanding. Then he pointed toward his truck. "Go get in my truck," he said.

Wendy wasted no time hightailing it to the truck and climbing into the passenger seat.

Kit then turned to the kneeling Mack.

"We're leaving. My advice to you is to stay down on your knees where you belong until we are long gone. If I ever see you again, I'll shoot your nuts off. Do you understand?" asked Kit.

"Yes sir," croaked out of Mack's mouth.

Kit returned to the truck, started the engine, and then drove out of the campground and headed for the sheriff's office.

Chapter Two

Kit drove in silence. Young Wendy sat in the passenger seat, sobbing softly to herself with her arms wrapped around her thin body. When they reached the parking lot of the sheriff's office, Kit parked the truck and turned to Wendy.

"I'm taking you into the sheriff's office and turning you over to the local authorities. I'll call your parents, and they'll then call the sheriff's office. The sheriff's people will make arrangements for you until your parents get here to take you home. Do you understand what I just told you, Wendy?" asked Kit.

"Yes sir," said Wendy softly.

"Good, now let's get out of the truck and go into the sheriff's office, and I'll do the talking. If they ask you any questions, give them a truthful answer. Can you do that, Wendy?" asked Kit.

"Yes sir," Wendy replied.

"Good," responded Kit, and he climbed out of the cab of the truck. Wendy exited the passenger side and followed Kit into the reception area of the sheriff's office.

Wendy stood by Kit's side, her eyes downcast, as Kit explained his visit to the receptionist. A deputy quickly appeared and led them into a small conference room. Kit provided the deputy with his identification papers and explained who Wendy was and why they were there. The deputy excused himself and shortly reappeared with a female deputy who sat next to Wendy. The deputy asked Kit to follow him to a separate room and had Kit give him a statement.

Kit was not surprised the deputies had separated him and Wendy. It was standard procedure, so each of the suspects could be questioned separately to make sure their stories were on the same page. The entire process took almost two hours. When it was over, and the deputy was escorting Kit to the reception area, he asked to be able to say goodbye to Wendy. The deputy smiled and said, "She asked to be able to say goodbye to you."

The female deputy brought Wendy out to the reception area and without any warning, she ran forward and practically leaped into Kit's arms. "Thank you, thank you, thank you," she whispered into Kit's ear. Kit put her down on the floor and smiled at her.

"You're welcome. It was my pleasure," he said. Then he turned on his heel and walked out toward his waiting truck. He had to pass through a crowd of reporters and cameras to get to his truck. Apparently, word had gotten out about the kidnapped girl being found and rescued and the press was hungry for a hot story. Kit carefully threaded his way through the crowd of reporters and camera carrying people. Fifteen minutes later, he was seated at a local pancake house having an extremely late breakfast.

An hour later he was back in his motel room. Kit checked e-mails, texts, and phone messages. He had forgotten about the reporters. He turned on the television in his room and saw himself walking to his truck. Somehow the reporters had figured out who he was and what part he had in the girl's rescue after he was gone. Since his truck had been at the restaurant and not the motel, the media mob had missed him in their first pass.

He put the DO NOT DISTURB sign on his room door and called the desk to inform them he wanted no calls, no visitors, and no information about him given out to anyone without his express permission beforehand. The desk clerk got the message.

The emails, texts, and cell phone calls persisted. He ignored all of them. He sent a straightforward text to Swifty. "Job done. Damn tired. Call you tomorrow."

Then he undressed and slipped into his large comfortable bed. He was almost immediately asleep.

Chapter Three

Kit was awakened from a deep sleep by the ringing of his alarm. Then he remembered he had not set an alarm. He got up, grabbed the motel alarm clock, and pulled it up to his sleep filled eyes. The alarm was not set. It was not the alarm. Then he groped to find the light by his bed and finally managed to turn it on.

After adjusting his eyes to the light, he then located the source of the irritated ringing. It was his cell phone. It was still plugged into the charger, but it was not shut off. Kit grabbed the phone and stared at the tiny display. He recognized the number immediately. He hit the button on the phone and said, "Hello."

"Hello, hello. Is that all you got?" said his partner Swifty.

"It works for most people who call me at an ungodly hour," retorted Kit. "What the hell do you want?"

"Turn on your damn television," said Swifty.

"Why?" asked Kit.

"Just turn the damn thing on," replied Swifty.

Kit fumbled around until he located the remote control for the television and turned it on.

"Anything special you'd like me to tune in for you?" asked Kit sarcastically.

"Try any local news channel, you dumb tenderfoot," Swifty practically yelled into the phone.

Kit punched the remote and found a local news channel. He was about to make another smart remark to his partner when it dawned on him that he was looking at footage of himself leaving the sheriff's office the previous afternoon.

"What in the hell is this?" he said into the phone.

"Apparently you managed to make yourself real high profile during your little trip up to Montana," responded a sarcastic Swifty.

"How?" Kit mumbled into the phone.

"Word got out about the girl being rescued by some out of state bounty hunter and then turned over to the local cops," responded Swifty.

"How?" repeated Kit.

"Man, you can really be dense some days," said Swifty. "Something like that is big news in a small place like Kalispell, Montana. Plus, it's that kind of story those folks love, and they eat it up like cotton candy."

"Oh shit," said Kit.

"You got that right. If I, was you, I'd get my ass packed up and get the hell out of that motel before the news locusts find out where you are and descend on you," said Swifty.

"For once, I agree with you," said Kit, looking around his room and mentally beginning to pack up his stuff.

"Call me when and if you manage to escape," said a laughing Swifty. Then he hung up.

Kit jumped in the shower and then shaved and dressed. He tossed his things into his travel bag and headed out the door in less than fifteen minutes.

When he hit the lobby, it was packed with reporters and before he could retreat to the elevator, he found himself in the arms of two large deputies who escorted him through the mob of reporters and out to a waiting squad car. The larger of the two deputies deposited Kit in the back seat and the other deputy put his bag in the trunk. Then they roared out of the motel parking lot to the dismay of the crowd of reporters and camera people.

After they were clear of the motel parking lot, Kit looked around and said, "What's this all about? Where are you taking me?"

The smaller deputy turned around in his seat to face Kit. "We got orders to take you to city hall," he said.

"Why?" asked Kit.

"I got no idea, sir. But orders are orders and we're taking you to city hall," replied the deputy.

Fifteen minutes later they parked behind city hall in a parking lot reserved for law enforcement vehicles. Kit and the deputies exited the squad car and walked into the rear of the building through a service entrance. Kit looked around at the deputies with more questions written on his face.

"No reporters here," said the smaller deputy, sensing Kit's concerns.

Ten minutes later, Kit found himself in the mayor's office which seemed to be almost overflowing with local dignitaries and law enforcement personnel.

The mayor hustled out from behind his huge desk to shake Kit's hand and clap him on the back.

"What the hell is going on?" asked a bewildered Kit.

"Why, you're here for the press conference," said the smiling mayor.

"Press conference? What press conference?" Kit managed to spit out.

"Why it's not every day we have a hero in our midst," said the mayor. "We're here to introduce you to the people of Montana as the man who saved a young girl from certain death."

Kit looked at the mayor like he was an alien from outer space. "I'm no hero," Kit managed to spit out. "I'm just a guy doing a job he was hired to do."

"Just smile for the cameras and then you'll be expected to say a few words," said the smiling mayor.

Thirty minutes later, the press conference was completed, and Kit had managed to say a few words without embarrassing himself. Then he had answered a barrage of banal questions from the press. Most of the questions seemed to be the same with slightly different slants to them. Kit was grateful when the press conference was over.

The deputies drove him back to the motel. Kit grabbed his bag, went into the lobby, and checked out. No reporters were anywhere in sight. Kit returned to his truck and tossed his bag in the back seat. Then he pulled out his cell phone and did a short search for a source of food.

Chapter Four

The short search uncovered a place he had heard about, and it was in nearby Whitefish, Montana. Kit got on his phone and made a reservation for The Lodge at Whitefish Lake. He looked at his watch. He would drive to the lodge and have lunch there.

Kit exited his truck and then pulled out his gear to check if he had everything he would need for an extended hike in Glacier National Park. He pulled out the large pack Swifty had given him for Christmas. The pack was large and well-made and should hold everything he needed. As he was examining the pack, he found a small note signed by Swifty.

"Check out the bottom of the pack, tenderfoot," said the note.

Kit examined the bottom of the pack. Then he noticed the bottom of the pack seemed to extend about four inches deeper than what appeared to be the bottom. He carefully searched the bottom of the pack and discovered a hidden zipper. When he pulled the zipper the canvas material opened and revealed a hidden compartment. In the compartment were various tiny survival tools and materials. Kit smiled to himself. "Typical Swifty," he thought. Then he mentally took inventory of the hidden compartment's contents.

"Everything, but a gun," he thought. Then he remembered something he had almost forgotten about. He returned to the cab of the truck and after searching in the center console, he found what he was searching for. In a small, zippered case was a tiny five-shot North American Arms .22 magnum revolver. The gun was so small, it had no trigger guard and no visible trigger. When you cocked the gun, the trigger appeared and was ready to fire. He retrieved the case, checked to make sure the gun was loaded with five bullets, and exited the truck. He returned to the truck bed and slipped the tiny case into the hidden compartment at the bottom of the pack. Then he slipped out the Kershaw switchblade knife he had tucked in his left front jeans pocket. He added it to the compartment. Then he dug a backup knife out of his glove compartment and slipped it in his jean's pocket. Satisfied with his adjustment to the contents, he replaced the pack and returned to the cab of his truck. Five minutes later he was on his way to Whitefish and a luxury hotel where no one knew he was going to be staying.

On the way north to Whitefish, Kit saw a Cabela's store on his right. He pulled into the parking lot and entered a spot close to the store entrance. He had a few items he felt would be useful on a trek in the park and he pulled out a small notebook and pen from his center console. He jotted down the items he remembered and then tore out the page and stuck it in his shirt pocket. He replaced the notebook and pen and then left the truck.

The store was new and quite large. After a few minutes, he figured out how to navigate the place and he started shopping. He spent longer than he planned in completing his shopping list, because he kept seeing things he would like to have. After an hour he found himself standing before a clerk at a register in the checkout line. Kit paid for his purchases and exited the store.

At his truck, he opened the cover to the truck bed and removed his purchases from several bags. He placed each item he had purchased in the appropriate pack or storage area and closed the truck bed cover. Kit balled up the several sacks and walked over to a trash barrel where he deposited them.

Then he was back on route 93 headed to Whitefish and his destination, the Lodge at Whitefish Lake. Whitefish was a small town of about eight thousand. It was a resort town with lots of seasonal residents and was older and quainter than Kalispell. Kit drove slowly through the picturesque downtown and finally reached the lodge just a bit north of the business district.

He almost missed the sign for the lodge on the left side of the road. He slowed and made the turn into the parking area along the south side of the long, rambling lodge. On the south side of the lodge was Lake Whitefish. Kit parked his truck and made his way inside the huge double doors at the entrance to the lodge. A nicely dressed middle aged lady was at the main desk and she greeted Kit warmly. She confirmed his reservation, accepted his credit card and he was given a key to his room on the second floor.

Kit returned to his truck and pulled it into the nearest available parking slot. He grabbed his everyday bag and returned to the lodge. Once he entered his room, he was pleased with what he saw. The room was rustic, but genuinely nice and up to date. He placed his bag on a low counter and put his ditty bag in the bathroom. When he was finished, he made his way downstairs to the dining room. A nicely dressed young Black man greeted him and led him to a table overlooking the lake. The man handed him a menu and told Kit he'd return in a few minutes to take his order. Kit quickly perused the menu and made a mental note of what he wanted for lunch or an extremely late breakfast.

He spent a few minutes taking in his surroundings. He decided it was an interesting mixed bag of things, which he quickly labeled "Rustic Elegance." He noted there were only eight other couples and one lady alone occupying tables in the dining room. None of them had even bothered to look up when he had entered the room. He was curious about the young Black man who had ushered him to his seat. Black people were rare in Wyoming. He had assumed the same thing was true of Montana.

The waiter returned and Kit noticed he had a name plate on his black vest. The name on the plate was "Al."

"Are you ready to order, sir?" asked Al.

"I am," replied Kit. "I'll take three eggs over easy, hash brown potatoes, and three slices of bacon."

"Would you like anything to drink?" asked Al.

"I'll take coffee, with cream and honey, and a large orange juice," replied Kit.

"Yes sir," said Al. "I'll get your order in right away."

Kit had noticed a slight accent in Al's speech. He decided to ask about it.

"I notice you have a slight accent, Al," said Kit. "Are you from the U.S.?"

Al smiled. "No sir. I'm from West Africa and am here on a temporary visa," he said.

"Well, your command of English is excellent, Al. You do a lot better speaking English than I would trying to speak an African dialect," replied Kit.

Al laughed and departed with Kit's order.

Kit studied the lake through the huge floor to ceiling windows on the south side of the dining room. It was a very impressive view. He could see some clouds, but the sky was mostly clear. Most of the trees on the edge of the lake were evergreens, but some were deciduous, and they still held their colorful leaves. It was the middle of September.

Al returned with a large coffee mug, a decanter of coffee, small containers of honey and cream, and a large glass of freshly squeezed orange juice. Kit thanked him, and Al departed. Kit poured a cup of coffee and added cream and honey. He had recently tried to switch from sugar to honey but had avoided slipping back to his old habits when he made his breakfast order.

Kit took a long sip of his hot coffee. It was strong and tasted as good as any he could remember. Of course, most of his coffee came from a cheap coffee maker Swifty had chosen for the office. The rest had been cowboy coffee made over an open campfire, so the competition was a little weak.

Chapter Five

Kit finished his first mug of coffee and took a sip of the very tasty orange juice. He had just started to refill his mug with fresh coffee when Al returned with his breakfast. The aromas of his fresh breakfast were terrific, and Kit realized how hungry he was. He attacked his breakfast vigorously. He was just eating the last bite of bacon when he became aware of a very well-dressed older man striding toward his table. The man was wearing a dark blue suit with a red and blue checked tie. He was of medium height, had grey hair, and a grey moustache. Kit glanced down at the man's shoes. He wore expensive hand-tooled cowboy boots in saddle brown. Based on his eyes, hair and skin coloring, Kit guessed him to be Hispanic.

Kit sipped on his coffee and pretended to not notice the man approaching his table, but his eyes watched the stranger's every move. Kit's eyes scanned the man for any sign of a weapon, but he detected none.

The man stopped about six feet from Kit's table. He glanced around as if to assure himself they were alone in this part of the large dining room and that the lone woman near them seemed unaware of them, nor was she listening. She had her head buried in her laptop.

"Mr. Andrews?" the man asked.

Kit looked up at the man and set his coffee mug down on the table. The man was older than he first had appeared. His face was wrinkled with age, his skin almost leathery in appearance. He might be wearing nice clothes now, but his face reflected a hard life in the outdoors.

"That's me," replied Kit in an even voice.

"Allow me to introduce myself," said the man. "My name is Alfonso Cortez, and I have a business proposition for you."

"Have a seat, Mr. Cortez," said Kit as he gestured with his hand to the empty chair across the table from him.

"Thank you, Mr. Andrews," said Cortez. He pulled out the chair and seated himself, as Kit leaned slightly back in his chair and studied him.

Cortez paused as though he had something to say but seemed unsure about how to start.

Kit broke the awkward silence with a question. "How do you know my name?" he asked.

Cortez paused, and then answered. "I saw you on television at the city hall news conference," he said. "I am here on important business for my employers, and this business requires someone with specific skills. I thought you might be the man I am looking for based on what I heard in the press conference."

"What exactly are you looking for?" asked a wary Kit. There was an air of both arrogance and hostility in Cortez's voice, and it belied the smile on his face.

"I need a tracker," said Cortez.

"A tracker?" asked Kit.

"Yes, an experienced and accomplished tracker," replied Cortez.

"I think you have the wrong guy," said Kit.

"Why wrong, Mr. Andrews?" asked Cortez.

"I just arrived in Montana," replied Kit. "I'm from Wyoming. I've got zero experience tracking here in Montana."

"I know all about you, Mr. Andrews," said Cortez. "I've done research on you on the internet. You have a long history of success in finding things and people for your clients. You always are successful when others have failed. You have a reputation for honesty and thoroughness. You are very professional at what you do. You have searched in several areas of the country including Arizona, South Carolina, and of course your home state of Wyoming. You are no stranger to mountains and wilderness areas." Cortez paused.

Kit was puzzled and now more than a little curious. "Why me?" he asked. "There have to be plenty of trackers and guides in Montana, and they know the country. I'm brand new to Montana."

Cortez broke his silence. "I need a tracker who can track a dangerous quarry, not some dime store cowboy who guides greenhorn tourists on scenic hikes," he said.

Kit studied Cortez for a moment. The man's facial expressions and his dark eyes gave no indication of what he was really after, but they gave Kit small warnings of danger. Warnings he had learned long ago never to ignore.

"Explain what you need and why?" said Kit.

Again, Cortez paused. Then after seeming to collect his thoughts, Cortez spoke. "I am searching for a man," he said.

"A man? What kind of man?" asked Kit.

Cortez paused again, as he looked Kit directly in his eyes. "A man who has betrayed my organization. A dangerous and violent man who is a ruthless killer."

"A killer? You need law enforcement, not a tracker."

"No, Mr. Andrews, I need a tracker. My superiors have assembled a team to find this man, but they are not trained trackers and are not native to Montana or the American West. My team needs a tracker like you to help them find this man."

"What happens to this man if they find him?" asked Kit pointedly.

"Their job is to find and capture him and return him to Mexico to face my employers," said Cortez.

"Alive?" asked Kit.

"Yes, Mr. Andrews, alive," responded Cortez

Kit paused. He leaned back in his chair and picked up his mug of coffee and took a sip. Then he set the mug down on the table.

"You're barking up the wrong tree, Mr. Cortez," said Kit. "I find things and people for folks who want them found. You're talking about finding a killer in a wild mountain area so you can take him back to Mexico and have him face some kind of personal justice not supported by any law in Mexico or this country. I don't do illegal stuff, sir."

Surprisingly, Cortez smiled. "I am not surprised by your answer, Mr. Andrews. In fact, based on my research, I expected nothing less from you."

"Then why are you here asking me to do something you know I would turn down?" asked Kit.

Cortez slowly put both his hands on the top of the table where they were in clear view. Then he looked directly at Kit.

When Cortez finally spoke, he spoke slowly and clearly. "Here is my proposal, Mr. Andrews. We will get up from this table. Your bill has already been paid. We will walk out of the dining room, out of the building and over to where your truck is parked. You will give me your truck keys and one of my associates will drive your truck. You will get in the back seat of my vehicle with me, and another of my associates will drive us out of the parking lot to my temporary headquarters here in Whitefish. Once there, you will provide me with a list of everything you will need to supply yourself to enter Glacier National Park and track down your quarry. If you agree to this job, you will be paid the sum of fifty thousand dollars. Twenty thousand dollars will be deposited to an account of your choosing and the balance to be paid when the job is finished," Cortez paused.

Kit broke the silence. "I have all the supplies I would need in my truck. But I already told you I'm not interested, Mr. Cortez."

"If you refuse my offer, Mr. Andrews, you will be dead within an hour," said an unsmiling Cortez.

Kit's face flushed with anger. "What the hell are you talking about?"

"I just told you, Mr. Andrews. You have two choices. Agree to work for me or be killed here in Whitefish within the next hour," said Cortez. The phony smile on his face was gone. His face was grim, and his eyes dark. "Do not doubt me, Mr. Andrews. Look behind me over by the far window," said Cortez.

Kit looked over Cortez's shoulder and took in the dining room. In addition to the lone woman working on her laptop, he saw a young Hispanic man seated with his back to the window. He was facing Kit's table. The man had a white napkin folded over his right hand. In his hand was a black semi-automatic pistol with a bulky silencer attached to it. The gun was pointed directly at Kit.

"May I have your answer, Mr. Andrews?" asked Cortez.

Kit looked Cortez in the eye. Then he spoke, slowly and distinctly. "You made a mistake Mr. Cortez," said Kit.

"Mistake? What mistake?" asked Cortez, surprise on his face.

"If that asshole shoots me, you'll already be dead," said Kit.

"How?" asked a stunned Cortez.

"My right hand is on top of the table," said Kit. "But my left hand is under the table, and it's holding a Kimber semi-automatic loaded with .45 ACP hollow point bullets pointed directly at your groin, Mr. Cortez. He shoots me, I kill you."

Cortez allowed his surprise to dissipate from his face. Then he actually smiled. "I am not surprised, Mr. Andrews. You have lived up to your reputation, but your gun is immaterial to me."

"I'd say it was damned material to you," retorted Kit with anger in his voice.

"You can kill me," replied Cortez, "But you'll still be dead. I have my orders. You would be wise to accept my offer. Otherwise, both of us will cease living. To my bosses, I am disposable. I knew that when I walked into this hotel. If I, were you, I'd accept my offer. Better fifty thousand dollars richer than dead in some dining room in Montana, Mr. Andrews."

Kit paused. Then he spoke with a grim smile on his face. "At the risk of being called a racist, I believe what we have here is a Mexican standoff."

"Just agree to the job, place your gun on the table, lean back in your chair, and we will walk out of this place to live another day, Mr. Andrews," said Cortez.

Kit was silent for a bit. Then he let out his breath and said, "Deal." With that he lifted his left hand above the table and placed his pistol on the white linen tablecloth after placing the gun's safety back on. Then he slid the gun across the table to Cortez.

"Now what?" asked Kit.

"We get up from our chairs and walk out the door together until we are at your truck in the parking lot," replied Cortez.

Then Cortez took Kit's gun and slid it into the waistband of his pants and rose from his chair. Kit got out of his chair and followed Cortez out of the dining room and then into the parking lot. The young Hispanic man also rose from his chair and followed the two men out of the hotel. He was careful to keep a distance of about ten yards behind the two older men.

Chapter Six

Ten minutes later Kit and Cortez were riding in the back seat of a black Suburban. Kit said nothing and asked no questions.

Kit studied his situation. The driver was Hispanic and looked to be a well-built thirty-year old. Kit still had a hidden knife in his boot, but his instincts told him to keep his mouth shut and see what was going to happen next. Knives were no match for pistols. Ironically, he remembered one of Swifty's favorite sayings. "Never bring a knife to a gun fight."

Very shortly the Suburban pulled into a circular drive of a huge three-story mountain home. When the vehicle came to a stop, the driver got out and opened the door to the back seat of the SUV. Kit and Cortez got out, and Cortez led the way to the front door of the large house. Before either man could touch the doorknob, the door opened to reveal a young Hispanic man dressed in jeans and a checked shirt. A shoulder holster was in plain view holding a semi-automatic pistol.

The man held the door open, and Cortez entered followed by Kit. The door closed behind them as they made their way across a large entrance hall to a side room set up as an office. Cortez slipped behind a desk and settled into a large leather swivel chair. He motioned to Kit to take a seat in one of the leather fixed chairs in front of the desk. Out of the corner of his eye, Kit could see the Hispanic guard with the shoulder holster assume a position in the doorway of the office.

To Kit's surprise, Cortez opened a drawer in the desk and removed a four-page document stapled at one corner. He glanced over each of the pages and then slid the document across the desk to Kit.

"Please read the contract carefully, Mr. Andrews. When you are finished you may ask any questions you wish," said Cortez.

Kit read over the document. It was a little different than his own contract, but not much. When he was finished reading, he placed the document on the table and looked at Cortez. "I read it," said Kit. "Now what?"

"Do you have any questions, Mr. Andrews?" asked Cortez.

"It's pretty straightforward," replied Kit. "I lead your men to the quarry. Then they take over. I get twenty thousand deposited in my account now, and then the balance of thirty thousand is deposited when the job is done."

"Any questions?" said Cortez again.

"Not on the contract, but I'm going to need supplies and equipment for myself and the four men you noted in the agreement," said Kit.

"My men have already been issued the supplies and equipment they will need for five days," replied Cortez. "You will only require what you need for yourself. Make a list of what you need and give it to Roberto," said Cortez, nodding toward the armed man leaning on the office doorway.

"When do we leave?" asked Kit.

"You leave in thirty minutes," Mr. Cortez replied.

"I'll need to get geared up from my truck," said Kit.

"Roberto will accompany you," said Cortez.

"Before I go," said Kit, "can you at least give me the story on the man we are hunting."

"Of course," said Cortez with a grim smile. "The man you seek is named Patrick Gonzales. He was a former enforcer for my employers. He got careless and was captured by the authorities in this country. He agreed to give them information about my employers for a more lenient sentence. While he was being transported from the Montana State Prison, my men ambushed the transport and seized Gonzalez."

"What happened to the prison guards?" asked Kit.

"They were disposed of," said a grim-faced Cortez.

"So why is Gonzales on the loose?" asked Kit.

"He overpowered my men who were guarding him, stole their car, and escaped. Using the car's computer system, we traced the car to the southern edge of Glacier National Park. He drove to a trailhead not far from the west entrance to the park, abandoned the car, and disappeared," said Cortez.

"Do you know where in the park he abandoned the car?" asked Kit.

"We know exactly where," replied Cortez coldly. He reached into the desk drawer and slid a folded map of Glazier National Park across the desktop to Kit. "It's marked with a red X on this map."

Kit unfolded the map on the desktop and studied it briefly. Then he refolded the map and asked a question. "Is this for me to keep?"

"Of course," replied "Cortez. He glanced at his watch. "You'd best hurry, Mr. Andrews. You now have only twenty minutes before you need to depart for the park."

Kit signed the agreement and slid it back to Cortez.

Kit slipped the map into his shirt pocket and exited the office, followed closely by Roberto. Once at Kit's truck, he gathered his gear and laid it on the tailgate of his truck. He checked over everything and then pulled out the pack he had been given by Swifty. He carefully filled the pack with his gear and supplies and added food and two canteens he filled with bottled water. He was finished with his preparations under the watchful eye of Roberto with minutes to spare. Kit turned to Roberto. "Are you going on this hunt?" he asked.

"Si," replied Roberto.

"Let's get this show on the road," said Kit. "We're burning daylight."

Chapter Seven

Minutes later they left the big house riding in the black Suburban. In addition to Kit and Roberto, three other young Hispanics and a driver made up the team. Their trip took about half an hour. After approaching the park on the west entrance, they drove past the entrance and headed east until they arrived at the spot where Gonzalez had abandoned his stolen ride. The spot was a trailhead named Packers Roost located on the east side of Ousel Creek. The five men exited the Suburban and gathered up their packs and gear. Kit motioned to Roberto, and he joined Kit on the side of the well-worn trail.

"What?" asked an obviously impatient Roberto.

Kit took out his map and laid it on a large rock. He pointed out the trail they were on. "If our man started out here, he is likely to stay on this trail as much as possible. It's the shortest route to the Canadian border." Kit pointed to the map. "The trail splits after a short distance. We take the right fork." Kit looked up at Roberto. "He has a head start. What happens if he beats us to the Canadian border?"

"We have men waiting at the border," replied Roberto.

"Take a look at this map, Roberto. The damn border is long, wild, and there ain't no damn highways through it. Your man Gonzales may not be a mountain man, but even a greenhorn can find a way over the border in this park without being seen, unless it's by a squirrel. If we don't find this guy before he gets to the Canadian border, he's more than likely gonna be in the wind," said Kit.

"In the wind?" asked a puzzled Roberto.

"Gone, vamoosed, disappeared," said Kit.

"I understand, Mr. Andrews," said Roberto sourly.

"Call me Kit. Mr. Andrews is an unnecessary mouthful," said Kit.

"According to this map, it's a little over fifty miles to the border," said Kit. "Normally a man makes about three miles an hour hiking. But this ain't a simple hike on a flat road. Did the report say if this Gonzales had a pack?"

"The sighting report did not mention a pack or any other kind of gear," replied Roberto.

"From what your boss told me, he's got guns and knives," said Kit. "That means he's more than likely to steal what he needs from other hikers. I'm gonna guess he might make about one and a half miles an hour in this terrain. How long ago was he seen leaving his car and entering this trail?"

Roberto looked at his watch. "His car was tracked to the trailhead about two hours ago," replied Roberto.

"Do we know what he was wearing?" asked Kit.

"We do," replied Roberto. "He was wearing green sweatshirt and matching sweatpants."

"How the hell do we know that?" asked Kit.

"He was seen by a couple who were parked at the trailhead. He was wearing his orange prison jumpsuit when he confronted them with a gun. He forced them out of their car at gunpoint and took the sweats from their luggage," said Roberto.

"Did he harm the couple?" asked Kit.

"No," said Roberto. "He just took the clothes and the man's wallet and left them."

"I'd estimate he's about four to six miles ahead of us," said Kit. "We need to move as fast as we can."

"I agree," said Roberto.

"Have your men check their packs for comfort on their backs and make sure each man has plenty of water," said Kit.

Roberto's harsh expression told Kit he was not used to taking orders and certainly not from some gringo. Roberto finally nodded his head and then addressed the other three Mexicans. Kit noted none of them had said a word, let alone introduced\ themselves. He noted one was tall and skinny, one was short and overweight, and one was average height but bald as a cue ball. He gave them nicknames so he could keep track of them. Kit settled for Huey, Louie, and Dewey. Those were the names of the three young nephews of the cartoon character Donald Duck. After the men made a few adjustments to their packs, Roberto signaled the men were ready. Kit stepped out in the lead and the small column set out on the well-worn and well-marked trail heading north into the park.

Kit took the lead and very quickly the trail forked. Kit looked at his map and then led the men on the left fork, heading north. The trail was well marked, and it sloped up at a slight angle, but the walking was easy. After about four miles, the trail intersected with Lincoln Creek. The trail continued on the west side of the creek. After almost two hours, they came to Lincoln Lake, which was a generous name for a small pond. Next to the little lake was a rest hut. The forest service sign indicated it was Sperry Chalet.

Kit knew the team needed a break. They had hiked over eight miles and although the trail had been easy, he had learned not all his traveling companions were in great shape for a forced hike in the mountains. Roberto and Huey, the tall, thin Mexican seemed to be doing fine, but Dewey, the short, fat Mexican and Louie, the slightly overweight guy who was bald were not faring so well. Both were almost staggering on the trail. They had stopped frequently to take short breaks, and both were sweating profusely, even in the cool air of the park.

The chalet was just a rough timber A-frame with a porch. On the porch, taking a break, were three hikers. Two men and a woman, all of them young, were seated on the porch steps drinking from their plastic water bottles.

Kit turned to Roberto. "Stay here with the others, and I'll see if these folks have seen our guy," he said.

"I'll go with you," said Roberto firmly.

Kit smiled. Roberto obviously had orders to keep Kit under a close watch and talking to strangers without supervision by Roberto was not going to happen.

"Fine. Let me do the talking," said Kit.

"As you wish," said Roberto with mock courtesy.

Kit approached the hikers and greeted them. While they were friendly, the woman kept her eyes on the other three Mexicans and there was a look of concern in her face.

"Headed north or south on the trail?" asked Kit.

The tallest man, a redhead, smiled and told Kit they were headed south to the trailhead. He said they had started from the Going to the Sun Road and hiked south. He said a friend was picking them up at the trailhead.

"Have you seen many hikers headed north today?" asked Kit.

"Nope. Not many, but we've seen a few," the redhead answered.

"You didn't happen to see a guy wearing green sweats heading north today?" asked Kit.

"As a matter of fact, I did," said the redhead. "If I remember correctly, I think we saw him about three miles north of here."

"He's a friend of ours and we were late to the trailhead, so I figured he might have headed out without us," said Kit.

"Well, I hope you catch up with him," said the redhead. "He was really bookin' it when we saw him."

"Thanks," said Kit.

"No problem," said the redhead. "Well, we better shove off." He got to his feet and his two companions joined him, and they left walking south in single file on the trail.

Kit noticed the female, a short girl with blonde hair in a ponytail, kept glancing back at his group, a concerned look on her face. "She has good instincts," thought Kit. He turned and looked back at his companions. Even Roberto and Huey were sucking down fluids from their water bottles. Both Louie and Dewey were sprawled out on the grass, their backs to two small pine tree trunks. He took out his water bottle and took two swigs from it. Then he replaced the bottle in his pack. "We leave in five minutes," he announced to the rest of the team. His announcement was met with groans and looks of distain. Clearly his tough companions were not in the best physical shape. Kit grinned to himself. If they were tired from ten miles on easy trail, what would they be like when the trail got steep and rough?

Kit checked his map. The regular trail ended here at Lincoln Lake, but there was a path between it and the trail he was headed for next to Lake Ellen Wilson. The path was only about a mile and a half and then they would be headed north and soon cross over the Continental Divide at Gunsight Pass.

After the allotted five minutes had passed, Kit got to his feet and slipped on his pack. "Let's saddle up and move out," he said loudly to the four Mexicans. He was greeted with groans and lots of curses in Spanish. After a few minutes, the other four men had shouldered their packs and were on their feet. Kit turned away from them and headed up the path.

The path became steep in a hurry and in some places, the combination of grasses and small stones made the path slippery underfoot. In about ten minutes the path joined the regular trail, and the footing became better, but the trail remained steep. They passed Lake Ellen Wilson, which was more like a lake than the pond-like Lincoln Lake and it was long, extending from south to north with the path parallel to it on the west bank.

Now the trail was steep and rocky and consisted of constant switchbacks to allow ascent to the ridgeline. Although the actual length of the trail was less than a mile, the steep incline and the altitude combined to drain the strength from each of the men, including Kit. They made frequent rest stops, especially for Louie and Dewey as they were gasping for air and struggling to keep up with Kit, Roberto, and Huey.

Finally, they reached the top of the ridge and stumbled to a halt. All five men had dropped to the ground in semi-exhaustion. After about five minutes, Kit sat up and looked around. The trail dropped down out of sight behind a large boulder. He saw a rough sign next to him. The sign announced their location as Gunsight Pass. Kit looked to the north and saw a long and narrow body of water down below the pass. He pulled out his map and found his location and identified the water as Gunsight Lake. The lake was long and very narrow, the blue of the water contrasting against the rocks and grass surrounding it.

Kit got to his feet and oriented the map to his location. They still had a way to go before they came to the Going to the Sun Road. He glanced up at the sky to his west. The sun was low on the western horizon. He looked at his watch. He estimated they had about an hour of daylight left at best. They would need to push hard to make the lake before dark, so they could build a fire and make a camp for the night. Hiking at altitude and on the rugged trail was hard in the daylight and would be impossible in the dark.

Kit walked over to where Roberto was seated and kneeled next to him. Kit extended the map and put his finger on their current position. "We're here," he said. Then he moved his finger to Gunsight Lake. "This is where we need to get and make camp for the night," said Kit.

Roberto studied the map and then asked, "How far?"

"It's about five miles," replied Kit. "We need to hustle to get there before dark."

Roberto again looked at the map. He nodded his head in agreement.

Kit looked over at Dewey and Louie. Both men looked exhausted. Moving on with them meant moving slower than they could afford. Kit pointed to the two slowest men.

"I suggest you and I go on ahead and let the other three men follow. We need to get to the lake and set up a camp and get a fire started before it gets too dark," said Kit.

Roberto paused and then shook his head no. "No, I cannot allow that," he said.

"Why not?" asked Kit.

"My orders are to always have at least two men with you at all times," said a stern-faced Roberto. "Pedro is doing fine. The three of us will hike on ahead and set up a camp and the other two will follow."

"Fine by me," said Kit. "We need to move out now. We're burning daylight."

Roberto got to his feet and went over and talked in rapid Spanish to the other three Mexicans. Huey, who Kit now knew was Pedro, got to his feet and Louie and Dewey seemed to breathe a sigh of relief as they remained lying on the stony ground.

Chapter Eight

Kit set a brisk pace, and Roberto and Pedro struggled to keep up. Going downhill was a lot easier than the trek uphill had been, but it was still treacherous. The trail was narrow and had several switchbacks, not to mention it was uneven and full of rocks of many sizes and shapes. Kit estimated the pass was at about nine thousand feet, and the altitude didn't affect him much at all. For Roberto and Pedro, it was an entirely different story. Their breathing was rough and shallow. It affected their senses which included their sense of balance. Within fifteen minutes, Kit was almost fifty yards ahead of them.

"Stop!" screamed Roberto. Puzzled, Kit came to a halt and turned around to face the two Mexicans. He waited until they caught up with him.

"What do you mean, stop?" asked Kit. "I told you we need to book it to get to the lake before we lose the light."

Roberto struggled to get his breath. Kit noticed Roberto and Pedro had both pulled out semi-automatic pistols in their right hands. If it wasn't so dangerous, it would have been comical, thought Kit. Two thugs with guns and not enough oxygen to be able to accurately aim them, let alone be able to speak. He waited patiently for Roberto to catch his breath and be able to speak coherently.

"You cannot get so far ahead of us," Roberto almost shouted. "You must stay no more than twenty paces ahead of us."

Kit thought for a moment and then spoke. "How about I stay in sight instead. We need to get to the lake and get a fire going before it gets dark and if you take a good look at the sun, you'll notice we're runnin' out of sand in the hourglass," said Kit.

Roberto now had recovered his normal breathing, and he thought about what Kit had said. Then he nodded his head in agreement. He did not seem to want to waste his precious breath on something as meaningless as words.

Kit turned and headed back down the trail. About every ten minutes he would turn and check out where Roberto and Pedro were behind him. Then he would resume his pace and push hard down the mountain trail. After about twenty minutes Kit could clearly see the lake below him. He checked behind him. Roberto was about a football field behind. Pedro was nowhere to be seen. Kit grinned and pushed harder down the rugged trail.

Kit reached the edge of the lake with about eight minutes of daylight left. He quickly found a good campsite. He took off his pack and began to pick up dead wood below large pine trees along with some old driftwood he found on the beach. He had a quick firepit with a small fire going with only three minutes of daylight left. By the time Roberto arrived, he had a good-sized fire going and was busily gathering more firewood. Roberto staggered to a position near the fire and collapsed on the sandy ground, breathing heavily. About ten minutes later, Pedro appeared and collapsed next to Roberto. It was another half hour before Louie and Dewey showed up. Even at their slower pace, they too were exhausted and collapsed next to the brightly burning campfire.

When Kit had collected a sizeable pile of firewood, he found a place near the fire and unrolled his sleeping bag. Roberto, Pedro, Louie, and Dewey had dug into their packs and Louie was in the process of making supper from their supplies.

Roberto came up next to Kit and said, "You make your own supper." Then he returned to the fire.

Kit dug through his pack and retrieved his tiny collapsible stove. He extended the legs and set it up on the sand. Then he put twigs and leaves and pine needles in the firebox and lit them with a farmer's match. He took his small pot and filled it with water from his canteen. When the stove heated up, Kit placed the pot on top of it. He kept feeding twigs and leaves into the tiny firebox. When the water in the pot boiled, Kit took the pot off the tiny stove and set it on a rock. Then he pulled out an aluminum foil packet. He cut the top of the packet off with his folding knife, and then slowly poured the boiling water into the packet. He used a small wooden spoon to stir the contents of the foil packet. He sampled the result with the spoon. Satisfied, he let the fire in the small stove go out.

Then Kit took his packet and spoon and sat on the sand, Indian style, and ate his supper. He occasionally took a drink from his water bottle and finally scraped out the remains in the foil packet and shoved them in his mouth. He looked up to see Roberto standing a few feet away staring at him.

"Something wrong?" asked Kit.

"What the hell was that you were eating?" asked Roberto.

Kit picked up the now empty foil packet and looked at it. "According to this label, this was beef stew," said Kit with a smile.

"Gringos!" snorted Roberto, and he walked to the other side of the fire and sat down next to his comrades who were eating beans and tortillas.

Kit waited for the stove to cool before packing it away. After their meal, the Mexicans sat around the fire smoking cheap cigarettes.

Now that the stove was cold, Kit packed it and the kettle away. Normally he would leave them out for breakfast, but since he had no idea what might happen that night, he was playing it safe and being ready for a quick exit.

Kit unrolled his compact sleeping bag. He checked the sandy ground for stones and then dug out a slight depression in the sand for his hips using his bare hands. Satisfied, he unzipped his sleeping bag. Before he could slide in the bag, Roberto appeared above him. He was carrying plastic ties.

"Hold out your hands, gringo," said Roberto in a harsh voice. Kit obeyed and Roberto tied Kit's wrists in front of him, giving him some distance between the wrists. When Kit looked at the distance between the wrists, Roberto noticed. "It's so you can take a piss," laughed Roberto. Then he disappeared to the other side of the now dying campfire.

"Could be worse," thought Kit. He promptly fell asleep.

Chapter Nine

Kit awoke about dawn. The air was still but cold. He sniffed the air. He could smell remnants of smoke from their now dead campfire.

He sat up and looked around. The four Mexicans were still asleep in their blankets on the other side of the now dead fire. He got up, put on his hiking boots, and pulled his small stove and kettle out and soon had a fire going in the stove and water in the kettle. He got out a pack of instant scrambled eggs and one of instant coffee.

By the time the others were awake and up, Kit was eating breakfast and drinking a hot cup of coffee. Kit then set the stove and kettle aside to cool and walked over to the spring he had spotted that seemed to feed the lake. He filled his water bottles from the spring, added some water purification tablets and rolled up his sleeping bag. Then he packed his now cool stove and kettle and stuffed the empty foil packets into a side pocket in his pack and got to his feet.

Roberto and his three companions were just finishing their breakfast. "Roberto," shouted Kit. "Get them boys packed up. We're burning daylight, and we got a man to catch."

Roberto did not like being shown up by a gringo, and his facial expressions displayed it to anyone who might be unfortunate enough to be looking. He yelled at the other three, and quickly they were ready to resume the man hunt. Roberto walked up to Kit who was standing with his hands held out in front of him. Roberto pulled out his knife and cut the plastic ties off Kit's wrists.

"Thanks," said Kit as he rubbed his wrists.

Roberto mumbled something that could have been "You're welcome," or maybe "Screw you." Either way, Kit didn't care. He had his hands free, and he quickly pulled on his pack and got it situated properly.

Five minutes later Kit was walking briskly down the rough trail, his breath looking like steam in the chilly morning air, as the other four men followed in his wake.

The group had hiked for about three hours when Roberto called for a break. Kit removed his pack and scanned the valley floor in front of him. He could see it would not be long before they began to ascend the other side of the valley. He scanned the sky for any hint of change in weather. The sky was clear with just a few clouds and the ever-present wind was more breeze than gale. The temperature had risen a few degrees during their morning hike, and the sun felt pleasant on his face.

Kit scanned the faces of his four companions. They had made substantial progress since they had left their campsite and to Kit's surprise, they had met no other hikers. Louie and Dewey were sprawled out on the sparse grass on the side of the trail. Kit picked up a handful of the soil from the trail.

It was mostly decomposed granite, just like he would have found in the mountains of Wyoming.

Roberto was talking to Pedro and pointing to the north. He had his cell phone in his right hand. By his expression and the tone of the rapid Spanish he was exchanging with Pedro, he was not happy.

Normally, Kit would have asked what was wrong, but he had figured out Roberto could barely tolerate Kit's very existence as part of this group. Keeping his mouth shut unless he was asked a question was a better choice.

Finally, Roberto quit gesturing and talking, and Pedro appeared grateful for a respite from Roberto's tantrum. Roberto stalked over to Kit and slid the phone back into his shirt pocket.

"Show me where we are on the map," Roberto demanded.

"Of course," said Kit. He pulled the map out of his pocket and unfolded it so that just the necessary portion of the map was visible. Kit pointed with his finger to a place on the map.

"We're about here, just east of Florence Falls," said Kit. "We're about two hours from St. Mary's Falls. The falls mark the south end of St. Mary's Lake. The lake is big and extends northeast to St. Mary's, which is just outside the edge of the park."

"Where do we go when we reach this St. Mary's Falls?" asked Roberto.

Kit pointed to the map. "We hike northwest for a bit to the Jackson Glacier Overlook," he said. "At that point, the trail crosses the Going to the Sun Road. When we get there, we must decide if we follow the road to another north bound trail or stay on this one."

"How do we decide that?" asked Roberto.

"We question every southbound hiker we meet to determine if they have seen a Mexican in green sweats heading north," said Kit. "Hopefully, we find someone who saw him on the highway headed west or someone who saw him going north on this trail."

"Seems pretty iffy to me," said a dubious Roberto.

"If you've got another magic option, I'm certainly open to it," said Kit as he tried to keep a straight face.

Roberto scowled, turned, and stalked away back to where Pedro was resting. Pedro did not look happy to see Roberto.

Kit grinned to himself. Tracking was as much skill as luck. When you lose the trail, you move in ever widening circles until you find evidence of your quarry again. The Mexicans were hard cases, but they were not mountain people. They tracked their prey in cities and towns, not in a mountain wilderness. Nevertheless, he could not afford to underestimate them. He was sure they were hard and cruel men to whom killing came naturally.

Chapter Ten

A few minutes later Roberto scowled at him and then asked harshly, "Shouldn't we be going?"

"Let's move out," said Kit. As he walked, he noted the incline of the mountain path was getting steeper. Ahead he could see the path moving back and forth as the terrain became even steeper. They climbed steadily for an hour. The temperature at this altitude was barely forty yet sweat ran down Kit's face and he could feel it running down the middle of his back. The pack got heavier with every step he took. He paused in the trail and looked behind him. Roberto was about twenty yards below him. Pedro was more like fifty yards. He could barely see Louie and Dewey. Kit decided it was a suitable time for a break. They had only seen a pair of hikers so far. Two young men, skinny as rails, went past them in a rush as they were glad to be heading downhill. They had appeared so fast Kit had not noticed them until they were right in front of him. Before he could say a word, they were ten yards past and below him.

About twenty yards above Kit, he saw a small grove of pine trees with several large rocks strewn between them. He headed for the trees and once he reached them, he let his pack slide to the ground and took a very ungraceful seat on the nearest rock. He moved on the rock until he found what passed for a comfortable spot. Then he took deep breaths and looked around him.

Roberto and the other three Mexicans had reached Kit's resting spot, and one by one they dropped their packs and found a place to sit. Louie and Dewey didn't bother to seek out a rock. Both men just plopped down on the rock-strewn ground.

Gradually Kit's breathing returned to normal. He sat up straight and did a check of his surroundings. He couldn't see any sign of the trail past the stand of pine trees. What he saw emerge from the back of the stand of pines made the hair on his arms stand up at attention.

Slowly emerging from behind the stand of pines was a small, black bear cub. The cub had not noticed the men nor caught their scent. He was busy sniffing the ground looking for new and unknown things, including something he could manage to eat.

"Shit!" thought Kit. He knew from experience that a bear cub was seldom far from his overly protective mother. Sure enough, after about three minutes, the big mama black bear appeared behind the cub. Mama bear's eyes were on her cub, and she too had not taken notice of the five humans slightly down the slope from her and her cub.

"Don't anyone move," whispered Kit to his four companions. Only Roberto and Pedro heard him and turned to look up the slope where Kit was staring. Louie and Dewey were still out of it and trying to get to normal breathing while lying on the hard, rocky ground.

Pedro reacted first, springing to his feet, and drawing a semi-automatic pistol from his belted holster.

"Shit, shit!" thought Kit. "The idiot is going to shoot the sow, and all hell is about to break loose."

Before Kit could react and physically move to stop Pedro, Roberto realized what he was about to do. He reached Pedro first. He grabbed Pedro's gun arm with his right hand and pulled it down. With his left hand he smacked Pedro across the face and knocked him backwards. Mercifully, the gun flew from Pedro's hand and landed on the ground about five feet away without going off.

By the time Kit had gotten to the two wrestling Mexicans, Roberto had Pedro in a chokehold and both men were sitting on the ground in an odd form of embrace.

Luckily, all of this went unnoticed by the sow, who was screened from the tussle by the pine trees. In the meantime, the cub had become fascinated by a large Monarch butterfly and batted at it with a tiny paw. Soon the cub was following the butterfly across the face of the mountain, moving away from the five men. Fortunately, the sow was right behind the cub. Nobody moved or spoke for over five minutes. Even Louie and Dewey had become aware of their predicament and had allowed their fear to freeze them in place.

Finally, Kit got to his feet and with that motion, Roberto released his hold on Pedro. Roberto got to his feet, made sure the bears were out of sight, and then turned his wrath on Pedro. What followed was a lot of rapid Spanish that Kit could not understand except for a few choice curse words he had heard from sheepherders when things were not going well.

When Roberto had finally exhausted all the curses he could think of, he stopped and took a desperately needed deep breath. He had not quite recovered from his previous climb when Pedro set him off.

Kit let well enough alone. What happened with the Mexicans was none of his business. They were not his friends and never would be. Their problems were their problems. He had plenty of his own without the need to add more.

From his limited vocabulary of Spanish, Kit had heard enough to know Roberto was angry because killing a bear or bears would bring down the wrath of the park Rangers and thus the local and state police. That was the last thing he needed for this mission. Their job was to find their quarry, capture him, and return him to their bosses in Mexico. Anything else was a problem for Roberto and the rest of them. A gunshot was a serious mistake in a park where sound traveled for miles. In addition, it would put everyone in the park who heard it or heard about it on edge and alert. Tourists would see and notice everything, especially something a bit unusual, like four Mexicans being guided by a gringo.

When Roberto had settled down, he walked over to where Kit was sitting and perched himself on a nearby rock. He sat for a moment as if gathering his thoughts and then spoke.

"We need to move on," said Roberto.

"I'm ready if you are," replied Kit. "What about them?" he asked, as he pointed to the other three Mexicans. Pedro was sitting alone, brooding after his tongue lashing by Roberto, and Huey and Dewey were still sprawled out on the rocky ground.

Roberto snorted in obvious disgust. "They're ready whether they like it or not."

Kit got up, shouldered his pack, and waited for the others to do the same. When everyone was up and ready, Kit headed back up the steep mountain trail. He did not bother to look back to see how the others were doing. That was Roberto's problem, not his.

After an hour of hard uphill hiking, Kit called a short halt. He had managed to sneak a few quick looks back behind him and knew a short rest stop was in order as Louie and Dewey had fallen almost fifty yards behind the others.

During the short break, all the men removed their packs and sought a comfortable place to plop down on the hard, rocky ground. While they were resting, a small group of hikers came down the steep trail. Kit looked up and studied the group. There were six of them, three men and three women. All of them looked worn out, especially the women. The group stopped on the flat area where Kit and the four Mexicans were resting and dropped their packs and plopped down on the hard ground wherever they happened to be standing. It was obvious they were not in the physical condition needed for a mountain hike.

Kit got to his feet and walked over to the man who appeared to be the oldest and the most fit of the group. He went to one knee next to the man who looked up to see who was interrupting his rest.

"Tough hike?" asked Kit.

"You know it, man. I thought I was ready for this, but this trail has kicked my ass," replied the man.

"You're on the home stretch," said Kit. "It's mostly downhill from here and there are several good spots to stop and rest."

"Thank God for small favors," said the man. He was about forty, about six feet tall and looked fit. He had red hair and a nice red beard.

"Seen many hikers ahead of us?" asked Kit casually.

"Several," replied the red headed man.

"You didn't happen to see a Hispanic guy wearing green sweats on the trail?" asked Kit.

The red headed man thought for a few seconds and then looked up at Kit. "Yeah, now that you mention it, I did see a guy in green sweats. I thought it was kind of an odd outfit for hiking up here, but I've seen some real oddballs in the past day and a half," he said.

"How long ago did you see this guy in the green sweats?" asked Kit.

The red headed man looked at Kit and seemed to notice him more acutely than before. Kit assumed the guy's radar had gone off because of the nature of Kit's question.

"Why do you ask?' said the man.

"We are following a friend of mine, and he's kind of a kook," said Kit. "He's physically fit, but he's aways doing physically difficult things without a lot of planning or preparation. Taking a hike like this dressed in sweats is something I would expect of him."

The red-haired guy seemed to relax when he heard Kit's explanation.

"There's a lot of folks on this trail who have no business hiking in the mountains," he said. "I'm surprised more people don't get lost and die up here."

"You and me both," said Kit with a forced smile.

"I'm sorry, I forgot your question," said the red-haired man. "Running low of fumes with not enough oxygen."

"How long ago did you see my friend in the green sweats?" asked Kit as easily as he could manage.

The red-haired man thought for a bit and then spoke. "I'm pretty sure I saw him not more than an hour ago," he said. "He seemed pretty beat, even after hiking up here without a pack."

"Thanks," replied Kit. "I appreciate the information. Hopefully, we'll catch up with him soon."

"No problem. Good luck with the rest of your hike," said the red-haired man.

"Oh," said Kit. "One more thing."

"Sure, name it," said the red-haired man.

"Which side of the Going to the Sun Road did you see him on this trail? This side or the north side?" asked Kit.

"The north side," answered the red-haired man.

"Thanks," said Kit. "And good luck with the rest of your hike."

"I'll need it," replied the red-haired man with a smile.

Kit got to his feet and motioned to Roberto to resume their hike.

Once they had hiked out of earshot of the resting group, Roberto spoke.

"What did you learn?" he asked harshly.

"Our guy is about an hour ahead of us," replied Kit. "He's stayed on this trail after he crossed the Going to the Sun Road."

Roberto actually smiled at the news. "Excellent," he said and fell back behind Kit on the trail.

Kit felt the natural excitement of closing in on his quarry that comes with the chase and successfully tracking. He led his motley crew of Mexicans back on the trail and slightly stepped up the pace he had previously been maintaining. When you get close to the prey, you increase the pace, but avoid overdoing it and giving your position away to what you are tracking.

Chapter Eleven

It wasn't long before Kit heard sounds of vehicles on a highway. He smiled to himself. They were getting close to the Going to the Sun Road, and then they would follow the highway to the west until they reached a place called Packers Roost. Packers Roost was at the end of a very sharp hairpin turn called the Loop on the west side of the Going to the Sun Road. There the trail continued north toward Canada.

A few minutes later Kit and his party emerged from the trail to the shoulder of the Coming to the Sun Road. They paused on the highway and sat on a concrete and stone guardrail to rest and take a drink of water. Kit only allowed a five-minute break and he then had them hiking along the south shoulder of the road. They had emerged from the trail at the Jackson Lake Overlook where a sign indicated the spot and their elevation of 9,642 feet above sea level.

When the short break was over and Kit headed west along the highway, Roberto cautioned his fellow Mexicans. "Keep you caps low on your head and keep your head down. Do not look up at the drivers of the cars and trucks we meet. I do not want them to get a good look at your faces," he commanded. In response, each of the other three Mexicans tugged their hats down low and kept their eyes on the ground in front of them.

Kit kept up a brisk pace, and the walking was easy on the level paved road shoulder. They made good time and soon reached the Hidden Lake Nature Trail and quickly passed it by. Then they passed a sign indicating the Triple Arches, followed shortly by the sign announcing the Weeping Wall. Finally, they reached the sharp turn of the Loop, and Kit halted them at the trailhead called Packers Roost.

As soon as they were off the highway and down on the new trail, Kit wisely called a halt and they flopped down on the ground to rest and drink water. Kit glanced at his compass and then his map. They had made good progress on the highway, but he couldn't let it be wasted by a long rest stop. He glanced at his watch and decided to give them a total of ten minutes rest before resuming their hike.

The road had descended from the point they had entered it, dropping almost three thousand feet in altitude. The decline had helped the speed of their hike and eased the hard use of their lungs. While Kit rested, Roberto got up and came over to where Kit sat. Roberto squatted next to him and asked to see the map.

Kit produced the map and pointed out where they were currently located. Roberto traced his finger along the dotted line indicating the trail they were on as it headed north. Then he handed the map back to Kit and got to his feet.

"We should be getting close," said Roberto.

"Maybe, maybe not," said Kit.

"What do you mean?" said an annoyed Roberto. "We made good time on the road, and we should be close!"

"We made pretty good time on the road," replied Kit, "but we don't know how fast he was able to move. He is alone and has no pack to slow him down. We will know more when we meet some southbound hikers on this trail."

Roberto frowned, but he did not attempt to dispute Kit's logic. Instead, he muttered, "Si" and walked back to the other Mexicans.

As if by magic or an answer to Kit's explanation to Roberto, two minutes later a group of three hikers came into view heading south on the trail. They stopped next to Kit and took a break. Each of the three finding a place to sit, and they slipped off their packs and broke out their water bottles.

Kit got to his feet and walked over to them. He stopped in front of the biggest of the hikers, a tall man, well built, with dark hair and no beard, who was taking a drink from his water bottle.

"Tough hike?" asked Kit.

The man paused, replaced the cap on his water bottle and smiled at Kit.

"Yep, it's real tough going uphill, but coming down is not easy," he said. "Lots of steep areas covered with small rocks and plenty of hairpin turns. It's easier goin' downhill, but you still have to be damn careful."

"The Road to the Sun is just past us," said Kit. "It was a pleasant change from all that uphill stuff we were workin' on before."

"I look forward to that," said the man.

"Seen many hikers heading north on the trail?" asked Kit.

The man paused, tilted his head back slightly and then spoke. "A few, but not many. It's getting' a bit late in the season, and all the summer folks have been long gone."

"I have a friend who was ahead of us on the trail. Hispanic guy, medium height, wearing green sweats," said Kit. "Did you see him on the trail?"

"Sure did," said the hiker. "He was the last hiker we saw on the trail before we got here." The man looked at his watch. "I'm fairly sure he passed us just less than an hour ago. He was making surprisingly good speed, but he was not looking so good."

"How is that?" asked Kit.

"He looked worn out to me. His pace was none too damn steady and like I said, them small rocks on the trail can be treacherous," said the hiker.

"Thanks, and good luck on the rest of your hike," said Kit with a smile.

"You're welcome. Good luck to you and your group. My advice is to not try to rush it up the next couple of miles. The trail is trickier than it looks. Take your time," he said.

"You bet," replied Kit. He walked back to his group and spoke to Roberto. "Let's move out," he said.

The Mexicans all groaned and got to their feet and then slipped on their packs. As they walked north on the trail past the three resting hikers, Kit noted all the Mexicans kept their hats down and their heads low as they passed by. Soon they were fifty yards past the three hikers.

Roberto hurried up until he was next to Kit and after looking back down the trail to make sure they were out of earshot, he whispered to Kit, "What did you learn?"

"Our guy is still about an hour ahead of us, but they said he looked pretty worn out and the trail ahead is tough. If they're right, it'll slow down his pace," said Kit.

Roberto just nodded his head and dropped back to fall in line behind Kit. Kit glanced at his map. They had a long hike up and across Flattop Mountain before they reached the Waterton River.

They hiked slowly up the elevated sides of the mountain going back and forth on the seemingly endless switchbacks the trail took. After almost two hours, Kit called for a rest halt.

That's when the unexpected happened.

Chapter Twelve

The spot Kit had chosen for the rest stop was a flat area next to the trail that was about twenty feet long and six feet wide. The men each found a spot and flopped down on the rocky ground after removing their packs. Water bottles were then grabbed, and the sound of slurping water was the loudest noise Kit could hear.

Kit decided to extend the ten-minute break to fifteen and then push on north. He checked his watch and sat back against a rock, carefully taking small sips of water. After almost ten minutes had passed, Kit's ears picked up the slight sound of footsteps on the trail above their resting place. As the seconds passed, the sounds grew slightly louder. Finally, he got to his feet and tried to see what might be coming. Then he heard metal striking rock.

He relaxed as he realized the sound could only be made by horseshoes striking rocks on the trail. He was prepared to see mounted riders or a mounted park ranger. What finally came into view was about the last thing he ever expected to see on this trail.

Coming over the top of the ridge in front of Kit was a man leading a pack burro. The man was older, with a goatee like beard and a slouch hat. He was dressed in a red flannel shirt and old worn blue jeans held up by old leather suspenders. As Kit studied the man's face, he realized he knew the man. The surprise caused him to be momentary speechless.

The man walked to within five yards of Kit and stopped. His burro followed suit.

"What the hell is wrong with your eyeballs, Pilgrim," said the man with a grin on his face. "Your vision done got so damn bad you can't recognize old friends when you see them?"

Kit's senses took over from his momentary shock. He stuck out his hand in greeting.

"I apologize for my momentary lapse of good judgement," said Kit. "You are probably the last man in the world I expected to run into in the middle of Glacier National Park."

The two men shook hands, and the grip of both men's hands was warm and sincere.

"Don't feel too damn bad," said O. J. Pratt. "I ain't seen you in a coon's age. I never thought I'd lay eyes on you up here in Montana. Did they let you out of Wyoming, or did they finally get tired of your sorry old butt and kick you out?"

"Last time I saw you was up in the Big Horns," said Kit.

"Yep, it was. If I recollect correctly, I'd run across this camp of pretty bad hombres and then saw you on the east slope of the Big Horns. It seemed you were lookin' for them jaspers, and you done took off without so much as a howdy do," said O. J.

"You're absolutely right on the money about that," replied Kit. "We got into quite a tussle with some pretty bad actors who were gunnin' for my half-brother, but it all turned out fine."

"How is your half-brother?" asked O. J. "What the hell was his name? If I recall it was kinda like some old outlaw's name."

"His name is Billy," said Kit. "You must be thinking of Billy the Kid."

"Right you are, Kit," said O. J. "I met so damn many people up in the mountains, it's hard to remember all their dang names."

"If I remember correctly, Swifty and I first ran into you up in the mountains near Buckskin Crossing," said Kit.

"Yep, I recollect that myself," said O.J. "We had a bit of a tussle with them smugglers you ran across."

"What are you doin' up here?" asked Kit.

"Prospecting for gold and silver, like always," replied O. J.

"Had any luck?" asked Kit with a smile.

"Found a bit just northwest of the park, but ain't found no sign since then," replied O. J. "How about you? What in tarnation are you doin' hikin' way the hell up here in a national park?"

"I got hired as a guide for these boys behind me," said Kit as he gestured behind him with his hand.

"You a guide up here?" asked O. J. with surprise on his face. He knew Kit worked mostly in Wyoming and had never run across him in Montana.

"I was on a case up here and when I got done, a guy hired me as a guide for these tourists from Mexico," replied Kit.

O. J. looked over Kit's shoulder at the four exhausted Mexicans resting among the rocks. "Them boys look plumb tuckered out," he said.

"They're pretty adventurous for flatlanders," said Kit. "They've done pretty well for greenhorns."

"Where are you headed?" asked a now slightly cautious, yet still curious O. J.

"We're hiking up to the Canadian border," said Kit. "These men are meeting one of their friends up there, who will pick them up at the border."

O. J.'s eyes told Kit he wasn't buying what Kit was selling. Kit knew O. J.'s eyes had taken in the four Mexicans and studied everything from their boots and clothes to their packs, and he was suspicious about what he was seeing.

O. J. sensed something was wrong, and he quickly changed the subject.

"How's that old horse thief partner of yours with the goofy name?" asked O.J.

"You mean Swifty?" asked Kit.

"The one and only," replied O. J. "But the only thing that boy is swift about is booze and women."

Kit laughed, and O. J. joined in. Kit moved his eyes back toward the four Mexicans and then moved his eyes back and forth. O. J. moved his eyes up and down to indicate he got the message.

"You didn't happen to see a lone Mexican guy in green sweats on the trail, did you?" asked Kit.

"Friend of yours?" asked O. J.

"Nope, he isn't," replied Kit. "But he's someone these four are trying to catch up with."

O. J. nodded his head and glanced back at the Mexicans. "There's a rest cabin on the west side of the trail about forty minutes from here. I saw this Mex dressed in green sittin' on the porch there. He looked plumb tuckered out," said O. J.

"Did you talk to him?" asked Kit.

"He never even raised his head when Bessie and I walked right by him. I figured he ain't got time for me, I ain't got time for him," replied O. J.

"Probably for the best," said Kit. "How's the trail between here and that rest cabin?"

"It's a tad excitin' in places," said O. J. "There's a stretch about a mile and a half long where the mountain kinda rises on the east and crowds the trail over to the edge. The trail is on about a ten-foot-wide stretch of flat land, so it ain't unsafe, but I can tell you it's damn scary if you wander too damn close to the edge. Looked like about a two-thousand-foot drop straight down on the west side of the trail. I was keepin' to the east side of the trail, but the wind came down the side of the mountain from the north and damn near blew me over the side."

"Were you hanging on to the burro?" said Kit with a smile.

"Damn straight I was," replied O. J.0

"Well, I best be movin' on," said O. J. "I'm wastin' daylight standing here jawing with you about crap that don't matter."

"Are you heading straight south?" asked Kit.

O. J. paused before answering, as if he were reconsidering something. "I plan to head east once I hit the Goin' to the Sun Road," he said.

"Good luck with your gold hunt," said Kit with a forced grin. "You get to a phone, give old Swifty a call and tell him you ran into me," said Kit.

"If I find any, you'll be the tenth person I call," said O. J. "If I remember when I find a phone, I'll give old Swift a shout out." Then he pulled on the burro's lead rope and headed down the trail past Kit's group's resting spot.

Kit waited until O. J. was out of sight and out of earshot before he moved. He turned and faced the four Mexicans. Roberto was on his feet and making his way to where Kit stood.

"You did good, gringo," said Roberto. "I couldn't believe you two could possibly know each other and meet here on this miserable trail in the middle of nowhere."

"He's just an old prospector I've run into several times in Wyoming," said Kit. "Wyoming's a small state and most folks who live there know everyone else who lives there."

Roberto glanced at his watch. "We need to get moving," he said. "I don't want our quarry to be gaining any ground on us."

"On your feet," said Kit. "We're moving out."

With assorted groans and curses in Spanish, the other Mexicans got to their feet. They pulled on their packs and followed Kit and Roberto back onto the northbound trail.

Chapter Thirteen

Kit led the way, and the group made their way up one switchback after another, as they ascended higher and higher up the terrain. After about twenty minutes, Kit noticed the trail changed. The mountain rose on their east side and the trail narrowed. Soon they had a stone wall on their right and the flat area left for the trail was only about ten yards wide. At the left edge of the trail the mountain dropped off and as O. J. had noted. It appeared to be about a two-thousand-foot drop straight down.

Ten yards gave the party plenty of room to walk on the side of the trail, but the wind had picked up and was blowing hard from the northwest. The wind forced the hikers to keep their heads down to prevent airborne dirt and debris from getting into their eyes. After walking about half a mile, Kit called a rest stop, and the Mexicans gratefully threw themselves on the ground without bothering to take their packs off. They looked like a bunch of dark-skinned turtles thrashing around on their backs on the rocky soil.

Roberto finally got to his knees and crawled over to where Kit sat.

"We need more rest," he told Kit.

"I agree," said Kit. "We'll spend fifteen minutes here and hope this damn wind dies down."

Roberto nodded and crawled back to his prone companions.

Kit sat on a flat rock with his back to the northwest to shield himself from the wind. The sun was out, but it was barely forty degrees out and the wind made the temperature seem even lower. He felt his body begin to stiffen from the cold and the wind. He closed his eyes and thought about his encounter with O. J. He knew O. J. was no fool, but he was unsure of how O. J. would be able to help him.

Kit's thoughts were interrupted by screams and yells in rapid Spanish he could not understand. He turned and looked behind him to where the Mexicans had been sprawled out on the rocky ground. All four of them were now on their feet, waving their arms and yelling curses in Spanish.

Kit got to his feet and looked to the north on the trail. About thirty yards north and above them stood a huge bull moose. He was in the middle of the trail and staring at the excited Mexicans. The moose moved his head slightly, but otherwise he held his ground and stared at the excited men.

"Shut up," yelled Kit at the top of his voice. "Shut up, you fools. You'll just piss him off, and God knows what he'll do then."

The Mexicans seemed to hear and understand Kit's loud command. All four of them immediately shut up.

"Do not move," said Kit. "Do not do anything to piss the moose off. Stand still and keep your mouths shut."

"What do we do?" asked Roberto in a loud stage whisper.

"Just what I said," replied Kit in a normal voice, hoping to keep the Mexicans calm.

"For how long?" asked Roberto again.

"Until the moose gets bored and moves on," replied Kit.

"But we are wasting time just standing here!" exclaimed Roberto.

"You do not want to mess with a bull moose," replied Kit in an even voice. "He's about the size of a John Deere tractor and a lot stronger. He's not afraid of you, me, or the whole bunch of us. A moose does what he wants to do, and we stay out of his way and let him do as he pleases."

"But our quarry is getting away," complained Roberto. "And according to the burro man we are getting close to him."

"I don't think you understand," said Kit. "The moose does not fear us. He can get angry easily, and he is extremely dangerous if he gets angry. Do not make him mad."

Ten more minutes passed, and the moose remained rooted to his spot on the trail, blocking their path to the north.

Then Pedro got antsy and moved to his left, toward the edge of the trail. The moose moved his head to follow Pedro's progress but did not move from his spot.

"I said don't move," said Kit firmly.

"Pedro has moved, and the moose has done nothing," said Roberto. "He looks bored, not angry. I think we can move around him to the west side of the trail, and he won't bother us."

"He looks harmless, but a bull moose is unpredictable," cautioned Kit. "Do not try to go around him."

"All he's done is look at Pedro," said Roberto. "I think this moose is one of the stupid ones."

The other three Mexicans laughed. They had become relaxed after their original fear of the giant beast when he first appeared. The longer the moose stood in the middle of the trail, doing nothing, the less afraid of him they became.

Pedro yelled something in Spanish at the moose, who just stared at him and remained still. Then Louie and Dewey started yelling curses in Spanish at the moose, who just stared at them.

Pedro, Dewey, and Louie began slowly moving to their left, toward the edge of the trail, heading for the space between the moose and the edge of the mountain. They were all yelling curses and insults at the moose as they moved slowly between him and the edge of the cliff where the trail rested on. Roberto remained standing where he had originally been sitting. He was carefully watching the moose. He had obviously lost his fear of the huge animal but was being cautious until he was sure the moose did not represent any form of real danger to him and his crew.

Kit realized the Mexicans were ignoring his pleas and he just stood silently, watching to see how the bull moose would react to the yelling, cursing, and the slow movement to his right flank by the three Mexicans. He hoped the moose would ignore the Mexicans, but he feared the worse. Every encounter he had previously had with a moose had been uneventful, but usually because he was on horseback and the horse wanted nothing to do with a moose and immediately veered away from any moose he had come upon.

The three Mexicans had moved slowly and were now perpendicular to the moose, walking slowly directly between the moose and the edge of the cliff where the trail was.

Kit held his breath. Maybe this moose was bored, maybe he didn't give a crap about Mexicans who yelled and invaded his private space. Maybe he was tired. Any of those options would have been fine with Kit.

The moose wasn't bored or tired. He was pissed.

Suddenly, without any warning sign, the moose lowered his head with his huge rack of horns and charged the three Mexicans to his right. The Mexicans barely had time to scream, let along move out of the moose's path before he was on them. His head down and his spoons deployed, he charged. He hit Louie first and tossed him into the air. Then he hit Dewey and Pedro both at the same time, and they were suddenly airborne as well. The moose had charged them a bit too hard. As the three Mexicans were tossed in the air, bounced on the ground and then were airborne two thousand feet above the canyon below, the moose slipped on the loose rock, and he followed them over the edge of the cliff and down to the canyon floor.

Suddenly it was silent. No more curses and screams in Spanish. No more snorting from the moose. Even the wind had stopped blowing. Kit and Roberto were too stunned to move or say anything

Chapter Fourteen

Kit didn't remember moving or walking, but he found himself standing at the edge of the cliff, staring down at the canyon floor, two thousand feet below him. He was soon joined by Roberto, who was also stunned into silence, shocked by what had just happened.

Kit peered down into the canyon trying to see the small objects on the canyon floor. He could not make out any details at that distance. He then remembered his pack and retrieved it. After a short search, he produced his small binoculars and returned to the edge of the cliff. He brought the binoculars up to his eyes and adjusted them as he stared down into the abyss of the canyon. He could just make out the small, crumpled forms of the three Mexicans. The larger moose was even harder to find because his color blended in with the canyon floor. He located the moose close to the bodies of the three Mexicans. The moose was closer to the face of the canyon wall, maybe because of his enormous weight compared to the three men.

Kit handed the binoculars to Roberto and pointed to the spot where he had seen the bodies. Roberto silently took the offered binoculars and brought them to his eyes. He soon located the bodies and let out a deep sigh. Then he crossed himself and made a silent prayer.

Roberto dropped to his knees. Kit knew it was killing Roberto to show weakness in front of him, but he understood. Roberto was in a kind of state of shock. What had just happened was shocking and horrible because it was so unexpected, and it happened so fast. Kit was still dealing with what he had just seen, and he had no real connection to the three men who had just plunged to their deaths.

Kit walked over to the nearest rock and took off his pack and sat down. He needed to give Roberto some time and some space and he knew it.

After about ten minutes, Roberto got to his feet, wiped his eyes with the sleeve of his shirt and then turned and walked over to where Kit sat.

"We must continue our hunt," he said simply and without any visible emotion.

"Do you have everything you need in your pack?" asked Kit softly. He didn't want to upset Roberto, but he had no idea how the Mexicans had divided up their supplies.

"I have what I need," replied Roberto tersely.

"Very well," said Kit. Then he pulled out his map and showed it to Roberto. "The next shelter is only a little over two miles north," said Kit. Then he pointed to the western sky. Serious looking dark clouds were moving their way at a good clip. "That's a storm headed our way. We need to beat the storm to the shelter," Kit said. "Let's head out."

They set out north on the trail, and Kit set a fast pace. He jogged for one hundred paces and then walked for fifty paces. It was a trick Swifty had taught him about how to cover a lot of ground and manage to keep going. He knew concentrating on the ground in front of you occupied your mind and helped keep unpleasant thoughts at bay. So did counting his strides and steps. After about thirty minutes they were about to crest a small rise. They were surprised to suddenly come upon half a dozen hikers walking single file and heading south. They were suddenly moving past them so quickly Kit barely had a chance to look them over. Four of the hikers were young men and two were young women. They all looked fit, and their hiking apparel and their packs looked new and expensive. As fast as the six hikers appeared in front of Kit and Roberto, they were quickly gone from sight. No one even had a chance to say hello, good-by or even howdy.

It wasn't long before the trail took them next to the small shelter. Kit and Roberto walked off the trail and both men let their packs slide to the ground.

Kit looked over the shelter. It was a log structure, about fifteen feet by fifteen feet. It had a roof and sides and a rough wood floor of planed logs. There was no glass in the windows, but they had wooden shutters that could be latched from the inside. There was a small pot-bellied stove in the middle of the shelter and a stack of split firewood was in an old wooden crate next to the stove. The stove rested on a hand-made stone base.

Along the walls of the shelter were crude wooden benches. Kit and Roberto removed their packs and Roberto sank down on one of the benches, his head in his hands.

Kit moved outside and circled around the shelter. He found a substantial wood pile and returned to the shelter with an arm load. He dumped the firewood on the floor next to the stove and turned to check out Roberto.

Roberto had not moved from his spot on the bench. Kit stood in front of him. "We need more firewood. I saw a pile behind the shelter. You bring in more firewood, while I get this fire going," said Kit.

Roberto looked up at Kit like he was noticing him for the first time. Then he registered what Kit had said and he headed outside the shelter.

Kit laid a small starter fire in the stove and stacked small piles of firewood next to it. Each pile was of firewood pieces slightly larger than the previous pile. Kit had learned this trick from Big Dave to set up your progressive sizes of firewood before you tried to start the fire, so you would be sure to have the right fuel for the fire as it grew in size.

Kit grabbed a wooden match from his small waterproof case and lit the shavings in the middle of his small wood pile in the stove. The shavings caught and soon were burning brightly. Kit added more shavings and then small pieces of wood he had split off from larger chunks of firewood with his folding knife. He put the knife back in his pocket before Roberto returned to the shelter.

When Roberto returned with an armload of firewood, Kit had a small blaze burning in the stove. Roberto dumped the firewood on the floor and headed out the door for another load. Kit then went to the windows and lowered and latched each of them from the inside of the shelter.

Kit returned to the fire and added more wood. He had just finished, when Roberto returned with another load of firewood and dumped it on the floor next to the stove.

"Good job," said Kit as he studied the pile of firewood. "Let's get one more load inside. The storm will hit here pretty dang soon."

Kit and Roberto went outside, and each man gathered a larger armload of firewood, and they were at the front door to the shelter when the storm hit. Kit pushed Roberto inside and followed him in. Kit slammed the door shut behind them, and the two men dumped their firewood on the shelter floor.

The small shelter seemed to slightly rock in the high winds that accompanied the rainstorm. The rain hit the shelter hard and sounded like tiny rocks hitting the sides and roof of the uninsulated shelter. Roberto dropped to the floor and sat cross legged next to the now warm stove. Kit checked the stove and added a couple of chunks of firewood. Then he closed the small iron door. He noted the small stove had flat areas on it's top, around the stove pipe that channeled smoke and heat out through the roof. The flat areas were large enough for a medium sized pan.

Kit went to his pack and rummaged through it. He produced his small one-handle pot for boiling water and added water to it. Then he placed the pot on top of the stove. Further rummaging produced two packets of chili in their self-cooking foil packets. He dug out his dining utensil that looked like a folding knife, but was both a knife, and a spork. A spork was a spoon with sharp ridges that could be used as a fork. Then he found the small packet that held several items including several plastic spoons. He extracted one spoon and then set the items on a bench.

During all this Roberto had not moved from his spot on the shelter floor. "He's in some kind of shock," thought Kit. He decided the best thing to do was leave him alone unless it was absolutely necessary.

Kit opened the stove door, as it provided some light in what was now a dark shelter interior. He got out his small hand-cranked portable light and unfolded the crank. He began turning the crank and when he felt he had cranked enough, he sat the light on the floor by the stove and turned it on.

Kit checked the one handle pot and saw the water was now boiling. He got out a metal folding cup and opened it. Then he poured the right amount of boiling water into the cup and put the pot back on the stove. Kit cut open the foil packets and held one open as he poured the boiling water from the cup into the packet. He grabbed a small wooden spoon from his pack and began stirring the water and the dried chili concoction in the packet.

Satisfied, he sat the packet carefully on the old wooden floor, so that it created a flat bottom and stayed upright. He measured out another amount of boiling water into his cup and then added it to the second packet. Again, he used the wooden spoon and stirred the packets contents. When he was done, he sat the packet down next to the first packet and licked the spoon clean and put it back in the pack.

"Roberto," said Kit in a loud, but not rough voice. Roberto seemed to wake from his stupor and looked up and then around the poorly lit interior of the shelter.

"Supper," said Kit, as he pointed to the packet on the floor and handed Roberto the plastic spoon. Roberto seemed confused at first, but then he caught the aromas emanating from the foil packet. He took the spoon, dipped it in the packet, and pulled it out. He sniffed the spoonful and then cautiously slid the spoon into his mouth. His eyes brightened and Kit thought he caught the hint of a smile on Roberto's face, as he then began shoving spoonsful of hot chili into his mouth.

Kit smiled to himself and slowly and deliberately ate his supper. When both men were finished, Kit took the now empty foil packets and Roberto's plastic spoon and folded them up and set them aside. He licked his spoon clean, dried it with his handkerchief and put it back in the pack. He would put the packets and spoon in the trash barrel, which sat outside the shelter by the porch steps, when they left in the morning. He and Roberto unrolled their sleeping bags and slipped into them. Then Kit turned off the small portable lamp.

Both men were asleep in minutes, the rain pounding on the roof and sides of the old shelter acting more like a mountain lullaby than the frightening noise of nature trying to attack them.

Chapter Fifteen

Kit awoke once in the night and rose to relieve himself. The storm had passed over, and the air felt cold and wet. Raindrops fell from the eves of the roof and the limbs of nearby trees. He retreated into the shelter and the warmth and comfort of his sleeping bag. The fire in the stove had gone out. Kit quickly assembled kindling from the pile he had made the night before and soon had it started again. He carefully added pieces of wood to the small blaze and quickly had a good fire underway.

Kit got up and went over to his pack. On the way to the bench where he had left the pack, he noticed Roberto was still in a deep sleep. Kit decided to let him sleep. He rummaged around in his pack and produced two packets of scrambled eggs and bacon and some instant coffee. Then he got the small one handled kettle and poured in a measured amount of water from one of his water bottles. He put the kettle on the stove and checked the fire. He added a few more pieces of wood to the stove and closed the stove door.

Satisfied with the stove, he opened the ends of the foil packets containing the dry frozen food and set them on the bench. Then he took out a tin cup and his folding cup and set them on the bench. He took two small packets of powdered coffee and added them to the cups. Then he set out his folding knife and spork and a plastic fork for Roberto.

When the water in the kettle began to boil, Kit took the kettle off the stove and carefully poured in a small amount of water into the two foil packets and stirred the contents with his spork until he was satisfied with the consistency. He poured the still hot water into the coffee cups and stirred them with the knife portion of his spork. Kit had made enough noise preparing breakfast to awaken Roberto. He had arisen from his sleeping bag and stepped outside the shelter to relieve himself.

When Roberto returned, Kit had breakfast ready on one of the benches with another bench pulled up for them to sit on. Without uttering a word, Roberto sat on the bench, picked up the packet of hot breakfast and stuck his spoon in it. Then he pulled out the filled spoon, studied it for a moment, and finally popped it in his mouth.

Kit watched as Roberto tasted the food and then chewed and swallowed it. He grabbed the coffee cup and took a long swing of the hot liquid.

"This stuff is pretty good," were Roberto's first words of the day. "What is it?" he asked.

Kit smiled. "It's scrambled eggs and bacon," he replied.

"Whatever it is, it tastes pretty good," said Roberto.

When they finished their breakfast and drained their coffee, Kit gathered up their trash and dumped it in in the covered barrel outside the shelter. Then he repacked everything and went around and opened all the shutters on the windows. When he was finished, he went outside where Roberto stood waiting for him.

Kit pulled out his map and folded it, so he was looking at the portion where they were located. "From here the trail goes downhill until it hits the Waterton River. Then it follows the river north past Kootenal Lakes and to International Falls. The trail should be easier, and we should be able to make good time. If we run into any hikers, let me do the talking. I need to know how far ahead of us our target is and since he's Mexican and you're Mexican, I don't want people to clam up just because they feel awkward. We'll act like you don't speak English. Does that work for you?" asked Kit.

"Si," said Roberto.

"Excellent," said Kit and he caught himself smiling for the first time in several days.

Kit led off, and they hiked at a good clip. The map was correct, and they were gradually hiking downhill. Most of the time that was much easier, but occasionally, the downhill part was steep and required several switchbacks to get through those sections of the trail.

They paused after almost two hours of hard hiking. Both men sat on nearby rocks, and each drank from their water bottles. The sun was out and although the air had a chill in it, the sun felt good on their faces.

While they were still seated on the rocks, a good-sized mule deer doe and two young deer came around a corner of the rocks. They were grazing on grass that grew in spots where the rocks had created sizeable puddles from the rain. Both men sat silently and watched the deer feed. The doe suddenly became aware of the men's presence, and in a flash she and the two young deer had disappeared back up into the rocks. Kit got to his feet and shouldered his pack. Roberto did likewise, and both men headed back down the trail.

After a bit, Kit could hear the sound of the Waterton River below them. They couldn't see the river, but they could hear the sound of water rushing over rocks.

Finally, the trail reached the river and followed it north. Kit led the way, and they pushed hard to try to close the gap between them and their quarry. Kit kept the pace as fast as he could, as the trail along the river was easy to navigate.

They came on the junction of Valentine Creek, and the river and kept up the fast pace. When they reached the south bank of Kootenal Lake, Roberto signaled to Kit he needed to stop and rest. They found a spot on some large rocks and after removing their packs, they sat down.

"Ten minutes," said Kit, warning Roberto that they had to keep up the pace.

Roberto nodded he understood. He was breathing hard. Sweat had soaked his shirt. The breeze over the lake was cold and between the wind and the sun, Roberto's shirt began to dry.

"Time's up," announced Kit and he got to his feet and the two men tugged on their packs and headed north on the trail on the east side of the lake.

When they reached the north end of the lake the trail began to rise and after half an hour, they came to another rough shelter on the east side of the trail. Two men were resting on the steps of the shelter. One man in his fifties and the other half that age. They were both dressed in good utilitarian clothing that was not new. Both men looked to be in decent shape. They greeted Kit and Roberto as they approached the shelter.

The two men got to their feet and both parties introduced themselves. The two men were Jacob and Jack, and they were father and son out for a fall hike. Both were from Kalispell.

"Do you hike this trail often?" asked Kit.

"We hike it about four times a year," replied Jacob, the father. "We prefer to hike it in the fall when there are less tourists in the park, and the trail is less crowded."

"We started at the southern border and the trail has been pretty empty so far," said Kit.

"We're headed to the Highway to the Sun where my daughter-in-law will pick us up," said Jacob. "As I get older, I seem to prefer shorter hikes," he said with a laugh.

"I understand," said Kit. "I'm a guide from Wyoming, and Roberto is my client for this hike."

"It's a great hike and a wonderful place to collect your thoughts," said Jacob.

"I certainly wouldn't argue with that," replied Kit. "We've been following a friend of my client and hoping to catch up with him."

"What does he look like?" asked Jacob. "Maybe we've seen him. We hitched a ride to the Canadian entrance and started our hike there."

"He's a bit of an eccentric," said Kit. "He's Hispanic and was wearing green sweats and no pack."

"We saw him," said Jacob. "He struck us as a bit strange. He had no pack, and he was wearing tennis shoes that looked pretty beat up and not what you'd expect a hiker up here to be wearing."

"You're very observant," commented Kit. "And you described him to a T."

"It wasn't hard," said Jacob. "He stuck out like a sore thumb."

"How so?" asked Kit.

"Wearing those odd green sweats, old tennis shoes, and he kept his head down and never looked up at us when we passed," said Jacob. "I said hello, but he just ignored us and plodded on up the trail."

"Plodded?" asked Kit.

"Yeah," said Jacob. "He was doing more plodding than hiking. He walked like a man on his last legs. I'd be surprised if he made it to the Canadian border gate. He was not in good shape, and his hair was matted with pine needles and small leaves."

"You're very observant," noted Kit.

"Spent three years in the army as an MP when I was young," replied Jacob. "You learn to spot details, and it's a hard habit to get rid of."

"I can only imagine," said Kit with a smile.

"Well, we better be heading out," said Jacob. "My son's wife Annie will not be pleased if we make her wait for us to show up at the road."

"How long ago did you see our friend on the trail?" asked Kit.

"Oh, about thirty minutes ago," said Jacob after glancing at his watch.

"Have a safe hike," said Kit.

"You too," replied Jacob, and he and his son headed south down the trail toward the Going to the Sun Road.

Kit joined Roberto sitting on the shelter steps. He took out a water bottle and took two swigs of water.

"He is close," muttered Roberto.

"Yes, he is," said Kit.

The two men rested for almost ten minutes and then Roberto started to rise to his feet. Kit put his hand on his arm and stopped him.

"Before we go on, I have a question," said Kit.

Roberto looked at him suspiciously.

"When we do finally come on him, what's your plan?" asked Kit.

Roberto's face relaxed. "It is good you ask," he said.

Then he looked around them, as if he was concerned about being overheard.

Kit almost laughed aloud. Here they were in the middle of Glacier National Park on a high mountain trail with no one within shouting distance, and Roberto was worried about being overheard.

"When we find him," said Roberto, "I will surprise him and overcome him with this." He reached into his jacket and pulled out a small plastic case.

"What's that?" asked Kit.

"It's a case that holds a chemical cloth that will make him unconscious when placed over his mouth and nose. When he is out, I will restrain him," said Roberto, pulling some plastic ties from his rear pants pocket.

Kit frowned. "After you render him unconscious and tie him up, what then?" he asked.

"What do you mean?" asked Roberto.

"We're in the middle of frickin' nowhere!" exclaimed Kit. "It's still miles to the Canadian border, and we're on a mountain trail. Just how do you propose we manage to cart him that far in this terrain?"

Roberto paused, as though he had just been hit by a heavy stray thought.

Kit groaned inwardly. An old, almost forgotten remark by his former roommate when they were in college leaped into his conscious mind. "Just got hit by a light of boltning," he used to say. It certainly fit Roberto like a glove at this moment.

"We need to discuss this more," said Kit. "Let's try to work this out while we walk. We're burnin' daylight just standing here with our mouths hanging open."

He didn't wait for a reply from Roberto. Kit picked up his pack and slung it on his back. Then he headed north on the trail. Roberto quickly grabbed his pack and followed Kit.

Chapter Sixteen

Kit kept to a strong, but easy pace and waited for Roberto to speak as they hiked north on the trail. They passed two more groups of hikers heading south on the trail. The first group was three college age men. They waved and passed by without any conversation. The next group was a man and a woman, both young, in their early thirties, resting on a log in the shade of an evergreen tree.

Kit stopped as if to rest and then engaged them in conversation. Previously when he had done this, Roberto had barely been able to disguise his disgust, viewing the stops as unnecessary and foolish. Now he understood the purpose, and he stood silently behind Kit as he talked to the couple. After a couple minutes, Kit said good-bye to the couple and headed back north on the trail with Roberto tagging along behind him. After they had walked for about ten minutes and Roberto felt they were safely out of earshot of the couple, he touched Kit on the shoulder.

"What did they have to say?" he asked.

"You were right behind me," said Kit. "Didn't you hear them?"

"The lady was very soft-spoken, and the man talked extremely fast. I had trouble hearing them and understanding what they were saying," replied Roberto.

Kit smiled and his face softened at Roberto's question and explanation.

"They saw our guy about twenty minutes ahead of us," said Kit. "They described him as looking like a homeless person who was down on his luck."

"When I get that worthless piece of crap back down in Mexico, he will learn what down on your luck really means," said Roberto sternly.

Kit did not respond and focused his attention on the trail ahead of him.

After about another ten minutes, Roberto spoke. "I have a question, Mr. Andrews," said Roberto.

"Call me Kit," responded Kit. "Everyone else does. It's easy to remember and even easier to spell."

That last remark brought a slight smile to Roberto's face. He considered his question before asking it to make sure it was said correctly.

"When we had the incident with the moose," said Roberto.

"Yes?" said Kit.

"You knew I was upset and shocked and yet you did not try to take advantage of me," said Roberto.

"Advantage of you?" asked Kit.

"You know, disarm me or throw me off the cliff," said Roberto bluntly.

Kit grinned. He paused a bit before responding to Roberto's question.

"I made a deal with your boss," said Kit. "I didn't like the deal or the way I was forced into it, but I made a deal. I always keep my word and that includes any deals I make with anyone," said Kit.

"Even when you were forced to make the deal?" asked a surprised Roberto.

"Even if I was forced. I didn't have to agree to the deal, but when I did, I gave my word and that's something I don't take lightly. Ever," said Kit.

Roberto walked along behind Kit, thinking about what Kit had just told him. Then he spoke again. "I was sure you were going to turn on me when we got to the shelter last night," said Roberto. "I was afraid to try to tie your hands, so I didn't. I thought you might overpower me and toss me over the side of the mountain."

Kit laughed. "What would that have gotten me?" he asked.

"I don't know," replied Roberto.

"I signed on to track this guy down, and that's what I intend to do. He's a criminal and an escaped one at that. I owe him nothing. I keep my word. When we do find him, it's gonna be your problem on what to do then. I only signed on to track him and find him for your boss," said Kit.

Roberto was silent for a few minutes, as he digested what Kit had just told him. He seemed deep in thought for about fifteen minutes. Then he finally broke his silence.

"When we find him, it will be up to me to capture, disarm and subdue him," said Roberto. "But I might need some help from you. Will you help me?"

"I'll help you, Roberto," said Kit. "But I'm not gonna lie or break the law for you. Is that understood?"

"It is understood. Thank you," said Roberto.

They hiked on and after a couple of hours, Kit called a brief halt. The two men slipped off their packs and sat on some rocks to rest. Kit produced a bag from his pack containing crackers and some hard cheese. They ate their light meal between drinks of water from their water bottles. Neither man had anything to say to the other. They were both tired and conversation was a useless waste of energy at this point. Kit checked his map and then showed it to Roberto.

"We are here," said Kit. He pointed to the spot on the map. "We are just south of where Olson Creek runs down from the northwest into this river. The junction is just next to Rainbow Falls. We are just south of Upper Waterton Lake. The international boundary splits the lake into a north half in Canada and a south half in the U.S."

Roberto studied the map. He pointed at a spot on the map.

"What is this Haunted Goat place?" he asked.

Kit looked at the point on the map Roberto was pointing to. Then he laughed.

"What is so funny?" asked Roberto.

"Goat Haunt Overlook is a campsite at the south end of the lake. Just east of there is Goat Haunt Mountain. I have no idea where the name came from or why," said Kit.

"Oh," said Roberto. "So, there are no ghosts?"

"Not that I know about," replied Kit.

"Good. I dislike ghosts intensely," said Roberto.

Kit just smiled. Then he pointed to a spot on the map. "When we get to this Ghost Haunt Overlook, we will be about five miles from the Canadian border," he said.

Roberto studied the map. "What is at the border?" he asked.

"I have no idea," said Kit. "I've never been there."

Kit took another look at the map. "It looks like there is a shelter located at the border on this trail, just past Boundary Creek."

"Will there be police at the boundary?" asked Roberto.

"Again, I have no idea," replied Kit. "Why do you ask?"

Roberto hesitated. He looked at Kit carefully for a minute and then he spoke. "Someone is supposed to meet us at this shelter on the Canadian border," he said.

"Who is this someone?" asked Kit.

"I do not know," replied Roberto. "I only know someone will meet us there and is to assist us in taking our prisoner out of the park and then back to Mexico."

"Then maybe we need to make this dude a prisoner before we get to the border," said Kit.

"You are correct, Mr. Andrews. The sooner the better," replied Roberto.

"Then let's get moving. We're burnin' daylight, and we've got a convict to catch," said Kit.

Roberto grinned, one of the first times Kit had seen him do that. They picked up the pace and headed north.

Chapter Seventeen

Shortly after, they were approaching the shelter at Rainbow Falls at the south end of Upper Waterton Lake. Kit could hear what sounded like loud voices coming from the shelter area. One voice sounded threatening. Another voice sounded angry. Kit put up his right hand to halt Roberto without speaking. Roberto stopped in his tracks and remained silent. He too, was listening to the loud voices coming the from the direction of the shelter.

Kit listened intently, but he could not make out what was being said. But he could feel plenty of anger in the tone of both voices. He turned to Roberto and whispered in his ear.

"I think we have found our fugitive," he said.

Roberto nodded his agreement. "Now what?" he asked.

Kit thought for a minute and then spoke. "I'll walk in alone as though I have no idea what is going on and distract this Gonzales cat and you slip in behind him and get the drop on him. He'll have his gun out, and he'll turn it toward the threat which is you. While he is distracted, I'll disarm him."

"How long do I wait before I move in?" asked Roberto.

"No more than three minutes after you hear me speak out loud," answered Kit.

"What will you say?" asked Roberto.

"I have no idea," replied Kit. "I'll make it up as I go and try to make it sound natural, but loud."

"Agreed," said Roberto.

Kit turned to go, and Roberto put his hand on Kit's shoulder.

"Good luck," said Roberto softly.

"Thanks," replied Kit. "I'm gonna need it."

Kit started walking slowly up the trail. He tried to make as much noise as would be natural for a novice hiker and threw in coughing and trying to whistle a tune he vaguely remembered.

Before he entered the clearing where the shelter stood, Kid stopped, removed his pack, and then unzipped the false bottom. He retrieved the knife and the small pistol. He checked the pistol to make sure it was loaded with one in the pipe. He secured the knife on his belt just behind his right hip. He slipped the small pistol in his empty right rear pocket, and he pulled out a flashlight like item in a sheath and slid it on his belt. It was a collapsible riot baton. He tested his ability to quickly draw out each of the weapons. When he was satisfied, he continued up the path and paused while he was still hidden on the trail by the trees between him and the shelter. He broke out into the clearing where the shelter stood like a sentinel on the side of the well-worn trail.

Up on the steps of the shelter were two young hikers, in their twenties. Two young men, both slim and athletic looking, and they had their hands in the air and were arguing with a shorter man dressed in green sweats and holding a large pistol on the two young hikers.

The hikers saw Kit before Gonzales did as his back was to the trail. Kit continued to slowly walk toward the shelter as if he had no idea what was going on and was confused by all the commotion the three men had been making.

Gonzales whirled around to see what had surprised the two young hikers and he quickly leveled his gun at Kit. Kit responded by putting up his hands as if in amazement, but he slowly continued to walk closer to Gonzales.

"Keep your hands up where I can see them, gringo," snarled Gonzales. He looked Kit up and down as if he were assessing what sort of threat Kit might represent. Kit did his best to look weak and confused.

"I don't want no trouble, mister," said Kit in the shakiest voice he could manage.

"Are you alone?" asked Gonzales.

"Yes sir," replied Kit as humbly as he could manage. Having a large caliber pistol aimed at your face tends to make anyone feel humble, so that part was not all fake.

"Do you have any weapons?" asked Gonzales.

"Weapons?" asked Kit as if he had never heard the term before.

"Yes, weapons, you dumb gringo," spat out Gonzales.

"No, sir. I ain't got no weapons other than this knife on my belt," replied Kit.

"Take the knife out and throw it on the ground in front of me," ordered Gonzales.

"Yes, sir," answered Kit. Then he purposely fumbled with the clasp on the knife sheath and finally pulled out the knife and gently tossed it handle first on the ground in front of Gonzales.

As Gonzales bent down to pick up Kit's knife, Roberto stepped from behind the side of the shelter.

"Don't move, asshole," Roberto screamed at Gonzales. "You twitch one muscle, and I'll blow your ass to kingdom come."

Gonzales froze in a bent forward position. He flicked his eyes as he tried to assess his surroundings and sought an opportunity to regain control of the situation.

"Drop the gun, asshole," shouted Roberto. "Drop the gun on the ground now!"

Gonzalez's hands were almost to the ground. He used his free hand to grasp at some dirt and leaves. His intention was to slowly begin to rise and act like he was going to toss his gun on the ground, but instead he planned to throw the debris at Roberto and then shoot him when he flinched.

As part of Gonzalez's ploy, he asked a question to distract Roberto.

"Who the hell are you?" asked Gonzalez.

Before Roberto could utter some semblance of an answer to Gonzalez's question, both men heard the noise of a metal snap. Then Gonzales was suddenly face down on the ground, his gun and the debris dropped from his now unresponsive hands.

Standing over Gonzalez's prone body was Kit with the extended ASP, commonly referred to as a collapsible riot baton, held firmly in his right hand. Kit knelt next to Gonzales and checked his neck for a pulse.

"Is he?" said Roberto cautiously.

"He's taking a nap," replied Kit. "He'll be fine in a few minutes, but he may have a slightly lingering headache." Kit got to his feet and told Roberto to use his plastic ties to bind Gonzales' hands behind his back. Then Kit took his ASP and pressed the top of the collapsible tool against a rock and pressed the handle down. The ASP collapsed in on itself, and Kit replaced the ASP back in the small holster on his belt.

The two young hikers came out of their state of shock that had temporarily paralyzed them when Roberto had stepped out from behind the shelter.

"What the hell is going on?" asked the taller one of the two. "Who is this guy?"

"Who the hell are you guys?" asked his shorter hiking partner. "What's the deal?"

Kit put up his hands to quiet them down. When they got quiet, he spoke. "This man is an escaped convict. State and local authorities are looking for him all over the park. He escaped from custody while being transported to prison, and he somehow managed to assault and kill his guards. We believe he was trying to escape into Canada."

The taller young man paused for a second before speaking, as if he were trying to make sense of what he had just seen and was now hearing.

"Well, if this cat is the convict, who the hell are you guys?" he asked.

"Good question," said Kit with a smile. "I'm a private investigator working with the local sheriff's office, and this is Roberto, my assistant. We've been tracking him for over two days."

Kit produced a business card and gave it to the taller young man. He looked at it carefully and then looked up at Kit with puzzlement in his eyes.

"This card says your office is in Kemmerer, Wyoming? How did you get involved with a fugitive hunt in Glacier National Park in Montana?" he asked.

"Another good question," said Kit. "I was here and had just completed an assignment and was asked to help out in tracking this fugitive down."

"Oh," said the young hiker. "I see." But it was clear he didn't really see much at all. After a close brush with possible violent death, he decided to shut up and move on.

"Holy shit," said the shorter young man. "Thanks for saving our asses from this freak lunatic. We owe you."

"You're welcome," said Kit. "Before you go back on the trail, let me get a picture of both of you and if you have identification, I'd like to take a picture of it as well."

"Sure thing," responded the taller man. "But, why?"

"You both are now material witnesses to what just happened here," replied Kit. "You're likely to be asked to come in and tell the sheriff's office what you saw."

"Sure thing," both men said almost in unison. They produced ID and Kit took pictures and soon both young and very relieved young men were back on the trail headed south.

Chapter Eighteen

Once the young hikers were out of sight and earshot, Kit looked over to Roberto. "Put our friend over on the steps of the shelter and have him sit down," said Kit.

Roberto grabbed a semi-conscious Gonzalez and pulled him to his feet. He frog marched him over to the porch steps and sat him down. Roberto sat down next to him, keeping his pistol nearby.

Kit walked over and joined him as he sat on the edge of the small porch. He got comfortable and looked over at a still puzzled Roberto.

"Okay Roberto, here's the deal," said Kit. "My job was to find this rascal and help you apprehend him. Technically my job is done. We have Gonzalez prisoner. We're just a few miles south of the Canadian border. I think it's time for you to tell me what the plan was once you captured this jasper."

Roberto's eyes brightened, as he realized what Kit was saying. "You are correct, Mr. Andrews," he said. "The plan had several options because we did not know when or where we would finally catch up to Gonzalez. There is supposed to be a shelter on the border, just west of Upper Waterton Lake. Border officials sometimes man it, but not always."

"Manned by who?" asked Kit.

"Sometimes Canadian officials, sometimes American, and sometimes both," replied Roberto.

"We are south of the border, and we have Gonzalez. Do we turn around and go back the way we came, or do we proceed to the border?" asked Kit.

Roberto was obviously surprised by Kit's question. He hesitated before coming up with an answer.

"I'm not sure," he finally replied.

"Hell, Roberto, none of us are sure of much of anything," said Kit. "We weigh the odds and try to make the best choice. That's what we need to do here."

When Roberto remained silent, an exasperated Kit continued.

"My job is technically done here," said Kit. "By the terms of the agreement I made with your boss, I could head back down the trail and leave you to figure out what to do next and nobody could fault me for not keeping my word."

Roberto finally broke his silence. "What you say is true, Mr. Andrews. You have done your job and more. I cannot deny that."

"But I'd feel like I left the job only partly done," said Kit. "I have no use for a man like Gonzalez. To me he is the scum of the earth, and the world would be better off if he'd died in childbirth. I also don't want your people coming after me just because they didn't manage to get him down to Mexico where he'd face your people's form of justice. I ain't perfect, but I keep my word, and I feel obligated to deliver this piece of crap to your boss."

Kit could see a sigh of relief visible on Roberto's face. Kit had him over a barrel, and he knew it.

Kit continued. "I want my job done and complete. I ain't interested in some hot head from your cartel to come lookin' for me to settle some imagined debt. I want to be done with all of you. So, you can count on me to help you any way I can to get this jasper out of the park and handed over to your cartel buddies."

"What are you proposing?" asked Roberto.

Kit remained silent for a bit as he collected his thoughts and formulated a basic plan. Then he spoke.

"Is someone supposed to meet you at the Canadian border?" asked Kit.

"Yes," replied Roberto.

"How many men?" asked Kit.

"No more than three or four," said Roberto. "The plan was to keep the number low, so it did not arouse the suspicion of the local authorities."

"Where was the proposed meeting place?" asked Kit.

"I was to meet them at the shelter by the border between the U.S. and Canada," replied Roberto.

"Are they Hispanic?" asked Kit.

"At least one of them will be from the cartel. Gringos he has hired may accompany him," replied Roberto.

Kit got out his map and studied it for a minute. Then he motioned Roberto over next to him so both men could see the map. Kit pointed to the map.

"We are here," Kit said. Then he moved his finger to the border. "The shelter at the border is here. The distance between them looks to be about five miles. Here is what I suggest. You take Gonzalez and find a good spot to hide far enough off the trail where you can't be seen, even by accident. You understand?"

Roberto nodded his head in agreement.

"There are going to be groups of hikers going up and down this trail. You need to be invisible to them. Do you understand?" asked Kit.

"Yes, Mr. Andrews, I understand," said a serious looking Roberto.

"I'll hike on up to the shelter at the border. Just one gringo hiking alone should not look suspicious to anyone I meet," said Kit.

"When I get there, I will check out the situation there. If there is no one there, I will return, and we will make alternative plans. If your people are there, they shouldn't be hard to spot. I'll engage them and bring them back here and let them take over our hostage," said Kit.

"I should get there in less than two hours. If your people aren't there, I'll wait for an hour. If they still don't show or there are lots of law enforcement there, I'll return," said Kit. Kit looked at his watch. "I should be back here within five hours. Check your watch."

Roberto checked his watch and noted the time. "Where should I hide with Gonzalez?" he asked.

"I don't want to know," said Kit. "If things go wrong, I can't tell anyone what I don't know. Watch for me on the trail and when you see me, call out and I'll join you."

"Okay," said Roberto.

Kit gathered his gear and turned to face Roberto. "Good luck, Amigo," said Kit and then he was headed up the trail. Roberto watched him until Kit was out of sight. Then he gathered his gear and prodded Gonzalez to his feet.

"Let's go, asshole," said Roberto as he pushed Gonzalez up the trail Kit had just disappeared from.

Chapter Nineteen

Kit hiked at a fast pace and reached the border shelter in a little over an hour. He passed about eight hikers heading south. Each time he met hikers he waved as he passed by them but said nothing and engaged in no conversations.

When he reached the shelter on the border, it was considerably larger and more modern than any of the previous shelters he had seen on the trail. Part of the shelter was an office like room with equipment to support its function. Kit saw solar panels on the roof and even the outhouse was more modern, including solar panels for light.

There was a group of five hikers lounging on the porch of the shelter. A sixth hiker was in an extended portion of the shelter that looked to serve as a small office for the customs officials when they were present. There was a border patrol agent inside the office talking to the hiker and there was another border patrol agent and a Montana state policewoman standing outside the office drinking coffee and chatting.

Kit made no move to join the hikers on the porch. He casually moved to an old stump under a large pine tree and removed his pack and placed it on the ground and sat down on the stump. He removed a water bottle from his pack and took a long drink. Then he replaced the cap and put the bottle back in his pack. He pulled out his map and pretended to study it. With the map in front of him he carefully surveyed his surroundings. He could see no sign of a cartel member. All the hikers appeared to be Caucasian. The two border patrol agents were white, and the state policewomen was white.

Kit decided to refill his water bottles and went to the water tank by the shelter porch. Two of the hikers nodded a greeting but said nothing to him. He refilled his bottles and then walked back to his stump and replaced them in his pack. He decided to wait for half an hour to see what might develop.

After about fifteen minutes, the six hikers had headed south down the trail. Two more hikers had emerged from the north and were in the small office with the border patrol agent. Both hikers were Asian, but not Hispanic.

After half an hour the two hikers were gone, heading south on the trail. Kit felt conspicuous as the only hiker hanging around the shelter and office and decided to head back down the trail south to avoid any interplay with the border patrol agents or the state policewoman. He was quite sure that normally there might have been one border patrol agent, but not two. And certainly not two agents and a state policewoman. They had to be there because they were looking for Gonzalez. His decision to come to the border shelter alone had been a good one.

Kit got to his feet, shouldered his pack and headed south on the trail. He walked at a fast clip and in a little over an hour he was halted in his tracks by hearing his name.

"Mr. Andrews," floated on the air. Not too loud. Not too soft, but with a distinct Hispanic accent.

Kit halted and looked around him. Roberto stepped out from behind a large pine tree.

"You moved," said a surprised Kit.

"I got anxious," said Roberto. "I figured it would do no harm to get closer to the border shelter and our friend did not object. Roberto grinned and jerked his thumb back in the direction he had come from.

"Any problems with him?" asked Kit.

"None," replied Roberto. "What happened at the border shelter?"

"Let's rejoin our package, and I'll explain," answered Kit.

The two men moved back behind the big pine tree and into a thicket. There on the ground with hands and ankles bound was Gonzalez. He was unharmed, but not very happy with his current situation.

Kit and Roberto sat on a fallen pine tree trunk, and Kit pulled out his map.

"The border?" asked Roberto. "Were my people there?"

"No sign of them," said Kit. "When were they supposed to be in position?"

Roberto looked at his watch. "They should have been at the shelter almost six hours ago," he said.

"Any reason why they would not be there?" asked Kit.

Roberto scratched his head and then answered. "None I can think of. But I was not given any details of their journey. I was only told when and where they would be located. After we connected, they were to take over the prisoner, and I was to follow their orders."

Kit paused to think about what he had just learned. After a couple of minutes, he opened the map and laid it across his knees.

"Did they tell you where this group was going to enter the park?" asked Kit.

Roberto thought for minute and then seemed to remember something. "I'm pretty sure they were entering the park at someplace where there is some kind of bridge," he said. "I remember, because we would be taking Gonzalez back that way to where they had their vehicles parked. They chose it because it was isolated and did not see a lot of hiker traffic."

Kit scanned the map and then saw what he was looking for. He placed his finger on the map and turned it toward Roberto.

"Could this be it?" asked Kit. "This spot with the ranger station named Polebridge?"

Roberto looked at the map and where Kit's finger was pointing. "I think that's it," he said.

"That looks like at least a two-day hike," said Kit. He looked at the distance scale on the map and measured the distance. "It looks like we're about forty miles away from Polebridge," said Kit.

"That's a long way," said a frowning Roberto.

"In the west, everything is a long way," said Kit with a wry smile on his face.

Kit grabbed his pack and began to rummage through it. He took a quick inventory and then turned to Roberto.

"Do you have enough food for two more days?" he asked.

Roberto grabbed his pack, opened it and began to sift through the contents. "I have enough for three days, four if I ration it," he replied.

"I have more than enough," said Kit. "We should be fine, even feeding our extra mouth," he said pointing to the still prone Gonzalez.

"I see several shelters on the way there, so there should be good opportunities to get water and the latter part of the trail has no shelters, but borders Bowman Lake for almost ten miles and then it runs next to Bowman Creek," said Kit. "Water should not be a problem."

Kit put the map away and then turned to face Roberto.

"The rules for this part of the hike are different. We must keep Gonzales' hands bound, but in front of him, not behind him. He'll need them in front for balance when walking. If he falls and gets hurt, we'll have problems we don't need at this stage," said Kit.

"I agree," said Roberto.

Both men looked over at Gonzalez. He just glared back at them. Hate filled his eyes.

"When we hear someone on the trail, either ahead or behind us, we need to get off the trail and stay hidden until they are well past us," said Kit.

Roberto nodded his agreement.

"The only exception is if you recognize them as cartel men. If that happens, it's your job to expose yourself and get their attention," said Kit.

"What about you?" asked Roberto.

"They won't know who the hell I am, and I have no desire to get shot by some trigger- happy cartel member. It's up to you to get their attention. When everything is good and calm you can introduce me and of course our honored guest Mr. Gonzalez. I'll lead, Gonzalez will be in the middle, and you follow in the rear. We need to keep at least ten yards between us as much as possible," said Kit.

Robert nodded his head to confirm his understanding.

"We have a long way to go and a short time to get there," said Kit with a wry smile on his face. "Let's head out."

Both men got to their feet, shouldered their packs and each of them grabbed one of Gonzalez's arms and jerked him to his feet. Kit headed south to the shelter where they had previously stopped. In a short time, they reached the shelter and encountered only two hikers headed north. Kit heard them coming, and he and Roberto grabbed Gonzalez and were hidden off the trail when the hikers passed. When

Kit could no longer hear them, he rose to his feet, and they continued their trek south on the trail.

Just south of the shelter, they took a trail to the east. This trail would take them to their goal Polebridge.

Chapter Twenty

The trail followed Olson Creek and after about five miles they reached a shelter. Kit had noticed two hikers resting at the shelter next to a small pond called Janet Lake. He used hand signals to have Roberto pull Gonzalez off the trail and into nearby bushes. There they waited until the hikers got to their feet and continued their hike to the east, back where Kit's group had just come. Kit waited until he could no longer see or hear the hikers. Then he rose to his feet and motioned for Roberto to join him. They paused briefly at the shelter to drink a little water, and then they resumed their hike.

After almost an hour, they came to a shelter next to Lake Francis. The lake was more like a pond to Kit, but it made for a peaceful setting. They rested on the steps of the shelter and Kit broke open his pack and made a quick lunch of cheese and crackers washed down with water.

Kit glanced at his watch. They had rested for almost fifteen minutes. He rose to his feet and shouldered his pack.

"Let's move out," he said to Roberto.

Roberto pulled Gonzalez to his feet and the three men set out eastward on the trail. They had hiked for almost an hour when Gonzalez asked for a break so he could take a leak. Kit had them pull off the trail and moved about forty yards off into some small timber. There they were out of sight from anyone walking in either direction on the trail.

Gonzalez leaned against a tree after relieving himself. Roberto then grabbed his arm and pushed him back towards the trail. He halted in his tracks at the sound of gunshots. Kit looked up in surprise. He froze in place and carefully scanned his surroundings. He could see nothing. More gunshots erupted, breaking the silence that had been surrounding the three men for the past hour.

Kit listened carefully. He had heard at least ten shots. Over the years he had come to recognize the difference between the sound made by various types of guns when they were fired. While distance did affect the sounds, most had their own special trademark noise.

He was quite sure he had heard pistol shots, but the last two or three shots sounded more like rifle shots to him. As he waited off the trail, the gunshots ceased. After almost five minutes and hearing nothing but complete silence, Kit motioned for Roberto to follow him back to the trail.

Kit had taken no more than a dozen steps when he heard the sound of feet running on the trail and what sounded like heavy breathing or sobbing. He immediately halted and held up his hand to stop Roberto's forward progress. The three men stood as still as statues, rooted to the ground on their position just off the trail.

Within a few seconds, he saw the source of all the noise on the trail. A tall young man dressed in a red shirt and tan pants came into sight on the trail, running like he was being pursued by the hounds of hell. He flashed by the three men's concealed position, never moving his head in any direction except straight in front of him.

No sooner had he passed than a second young man appeared, running on the trail, seemingly trying in vain to catch up with his more fleet-footed companion. A minute or two passed and then two young women appeared. Both of them were running hard and the one dark haired female Kit got a good look at, had a look of absolute terror on her young face.

Kit waited for another five minutes, but no more runners appeared on the trail and total silence once again dominated their surroundings.

Roberto tapped Kit on the shoulder. Kit turned to look at him.

"What the hell was that?" Roberto whispered in Kit's ear.

"I have no idea," replied Kit.

He waited a bit longer and then made a decision. Kit turned to Roberto.

"Take our friend back to the thicket where we were," said Kit. "I'll head down the trail and see if I can scout out what the heck in going on. Wait for me here and don't get careless with Gonzalez."

Roberto nodded his agreement and grabbed Gonzalez by the elbow and began to lead him back to the thicket they had just exited.

Kit waited until they were out of sight, and then he moved forward until he was standing on the trail. Once there, He paused, listening carefully for any sounds. Other than a breeze in the treetops next to the trail and the occasional bird call, he heard nothing that set off any internal alarms.

He was about to move out from behind a pine tree about five yards from the trail when he heard the sound of boots slamming against the ground. He stepped back a bit, so the tree trunk shielded him from view, but gave him a good visual slice of the trail to the west. He quickly was able to see a figure coming into view on the trail. He could see it was a young Mexican man, dressed in black, with a pistol in his right hand. The man was running fast, his head down, and breathing extremely hard.

Kit reached down with his left hand and removed the collapsible baton from its sheath and snapped it down. The baton automatically extended itself. Kit waited until the young Mexican was about seven yards from passing by and then he stepped out and wacked the man across the side of his head. The strike was effective. The young Mexican dropped to the trail like a wet sack of cement.

Kit quickly stepped out on the trail and rolled the man over on his belly. Then he shucked off his pack and removed plastic ties from it. He used them to shackle the man's wrists behind him. Then he shackled the man's ankles together. The final touch, which Big Dave had taught him years ago was a final plastic tie that connected both shackles together, effectively hog tying the young Mexican.

Kit stood up and then dragged the young Mexican to the side of the trail, but not out of sight of anyone passing by on the trail.

Kit looked down at his handiwork and smiled. This effectively left the Mexican to be found and picked up by the authorities and no one, not even the young Mexican, had any idea of how he got knocked down and tied up. Kit searched the ground and found the man's pistol on the trail. He kicked it off the trail and into some weeds.

Kit made his way slowly eastward on the trail. He kept to the south side of the trail, ready to disappear into the surrounding trees and brush if he chanced to meet anyone on the trail.

After almost half an hour of slow movement, he began to hear noises. Sound carries well in the mountains where there are few obstacles to its transmission. But, on this trail, the surrounding trees and brush often muffled much of the sound. In this case he was hearing voices and the unmistakable sound of some metal objects banging together.

Kit paused and again checked for movement, noise, or scents. He could still hear the voices and the sound of some metal objects hitting each other. He could see nothing. He took a deep breath and resumed his slow progress down the trail to the east. The trail began to slope downwards, and the voices got louder. Kit paused and studied his surroundings.

As the trail wound down toward the west, he could see the north side of the trail stayed level and thus higher than the south side.

He moved across the trail and made his way slightly north of the trail and then found a game trail that paralleled the main trail. He slowly and carefully made his way along the game trail, which was about twenty yards above the hiking trail and hidden by tall weeds.

Chapter Twenty-One

Kit moved slowly. Carefully placing each step where he wanted it to avoid snaping a twig or making any unnecessary noise. All this caution made progress slow and time consuming, but Kit knew from experience taking time to do things right was hands down better than blundering into something he might regret.

After twenty-five minutes of slow progress, Kit could now hear the voices loud and clear enough to understand most of what was being said. As he slipped past a large fir tree, he got his first real look at what was going on. He dropped down to his belly and wormed his way forward for about fifteen yards. From there he had a good vantage point with an excellent view of the trail about forty yards below him.

He reached in his pack and pulled out his set of small binoculars. He could see several men in uniforms standing around and talking. One of them was on what appeared to be a satellite phone. Sitting on the ground with their hands handcuffed behind them, were four young men. Two of the men were Mexicans and the other two were Anglos with wispy beards that looked more like crop failures then actual beards.

Kit studied the men in unforms. There were five of them, including the one on the satellite phone. Two had

Montana State Police uniforms and the other three were dressed in khaki shirts, jeans, and cowboy hats like the deputy sheriff he had dealt with earlier back in Kalispel. Kit studied the area around the men but could see no bodies or anything else out of place. He replaced the binoculars back in his shirt pocket and then reversed his position and began crawling back the way he had come.

When he got back to the big fir tree, he got to his feet and moved as quickly and silently as he could as he made his way back to where he had left Roberto and their prisoner. He got back to the trail in half the time it had taken to move down to where he could see the officers and their captives. Once he hit the trail he jogged back to the tree where he had previously entered the trail. Then he made his way back to where Roberto had been impatiently waiting.

"What's happened?" hoarsely whispered an agitated Roberto.

"Give me a minute to catch my breath," said Kit. He grabbed one of his canteens and took a long swig of water. After replacing the top to the canteen, he sat down on an old log. Roberto moved over to squat in front of him.

"What happened?" Roberto whispered again.

"Apparently the relief squad you were supposed to hook up with ran into some cops," said Kit.

"Cops! Out here?" blurted out Roberto.

"Yes, cops, out here," said a stern-faced Kit.

"But how?" asked Roberto.

"I have no idea, but I can make a pretty good guess," said Kit.

Roberto said nothing, but his face said it all. He was surprised, angry, and scared, all at the same time.

Kit reopened the canteen and took another long swig of water. Then he replaced the top and put the canteen on the log.

"What's your guess?" asked Roberto.

"I'm pretty sure those cops were out in force looking for this jasper," said Kit as he pointed to their bound prisoner who was sitting on the ground with his back against an old stump.

"I think they were coming up the trail from Polebridge and ran into your people," said Kit.

"Just by accident?" asked Roberto.

"It really doesn't matter," said Kit. "The cops could have taken a rest stop and your folks came up the trail and were unexpectedly face to face in the middle of nowhere. Your people were dressed all in black and armed. That's not what's legal or normal in any national park. It doesn't really matter who was resting and who ran into who. Either way there was a confrontation, and my guess is your folks panicked and pulled guns and began shooting and the cops shot back."

"Was anyone killed?" asked Roberto.

"Not that I could see," replied Kit.

"How many were in my people's group?" asked Roberto.

Kit thought for a moment and then he replied. "I think there were five in the cartel party."

"I thought you saw all of them?" asked Roberto.

"I did," said Kit. "I got pretty close above them and used my binoculars."

"Then why do you say you thought you saw all of them?" asked Roberto.

"I saw five cops at the clearing," said Kit. "I also saw four young men setting on their butts handcuffed. Two of them were Mexican and two of them were white dudes with wannabe beards."

"So, there were four in the cartel party?" asked Roberto.

"Actually, I think there were five in the party," said Kit.

"How so?" asked Roberto. "You said there were four."

"I'm sorry, I forgot about the first one," said Kit.

"First one?" asked Roberto.

"Yes," said Kit. "Before I stepped out on the trail, I heard this person pounding up from the west. I could see he was a young Mexican dressed all in black. He was bookin' it, and he had a pistol in his right hand."

"What happened?" asked Roberto.

"I used my collapsible baton and whacked him when he ran by where I was standing," said Kit. "He went out like a bad light. Then I trussed him up with plastic ties and left him on the side of the trail."

"Why did you do that?" asked a puzzled Roberto.

"I didn't want him to get away, and I didn't want to have to explain myself to a bunch of suspicious cops," said Kit. "I made your guy a deal and I keep my word. I want no part of what was going on west of us on the trail."

"So, no one will know how this man came to be tied up on the trail?" asked Roberto.

"Nope, they won't," said Kit. "I agreed to get this jasper to your people out of the park and I intend to keep my word, but I have no intention of getting cross ways with a bunch of angry and revenge fueled cops."

"Angry?" asked Roberto.

"You're forgetting our pal laying over there killed two policemen who were transporting him to prison," said Kit. "I can guarantee you the cops haven't forgotten."

Roberto was silent for a bit and then he looked up at Kit and spoke. "What do we do now?" he asked.

"The truth?" asked Kit.

"Of course, the truth," said Roberto.

"I have no damn idea at the moment," said Kit.

"Shit," said Roberto.

"Let me take a look at our map and see if we have any options," said Kit.

"Options?" asked Roberto.

"We got to play the cards we been dealt," said Kit. "I just need to study our cards before I can answer your question."

Kit pulled the map out of his shirt pocket and unfolded it. He located their location on the map and then began to study it.

Roberto got to his feet and walked over to where their prisoner sat against the stump. Then he pulled a knife from his belt and stared at the sitting Gonzalez.

"Maybe we should cut our losses," said Roberto.

"What do you mean?" asked Kit.

"Let's just kill this worthless piece of shit, take a picture of him with his throat cut and then get the hell out of this miserable place," said Roberto.

"That ain't my deal," said Kit. "I agree he's a worthless piece of shit and the world would likely be a better place if we did kill him, but I don't kill unarmed men, even one's like this who damned well deserve it."

"I'll do the killing," said a determined Roberto, his eyes full of hate and anger.

"You sure you want to do that?" asked Kit.

"I'm sure," retorted Roberto.

"Consider the consequences," said Kit.

"Consequences? What consequences?" asked Roberto.

"Your orders as I understand them is to capture this asshole, which you have done. Then to deliver him to the cartel folks who were sent to the park. Thanks to the cops that option is off the table. I assume you were ordered to deliver shithead to them alive and kicking. If so, your job ain't done yet," said Kit.

"What are you saying?" asked Roberto.

"I'm saying we need to get him out of this park alive and in one piece. Then you can contact your bosses and get him taken off our hands," said Kit.

"How do we do that?" asked a confused Roberto.

"I ain't sure," said Kit. "But if you'll give me a little time to study this map, I just might be able to give you a good answer."

Roberto shrugged his shoulders and returned the knife to the sheath on his belt. Then he returned to the log and sat beside Kit.

Kit ignored his presence and continued to study the map.

Roberto sat and sulked and waited for Kit to pull a rabbit out of a hat.

Chapter Twenty-Two

Kit studied the map for about ten minutes. Then he took another drink of water. He recapped the water bottle and then replaced it in his pack. He picked up the map again and began tracing his finger over it. He did this several times and finally set the map down.

"Well?" said an impatient Roberto. "What did you find?"

Kit looked up at Roberto and then over at their bound prisoner. "You ain't gonna like what I found," said Kit.

"Try me," said Roberto.

"We've got a couple of choices," said Kit.

"What are they?" asked Roberto.

"To be clear, both choices suck," said Kit.

"Why?" asked Roberto.

"Both cross the continental divide so we will be at high altitude," replied Kit.

"We can do that," replied an anxious Roberto.

"But both choices are without any known trails," said Kit.

Roberto looked puzzled at that remark.

Kit smiled slightly. "What I mean is that even though the distances of the shortcuts are not very long, they are very difficult."

"How long are they?" asked Roberto.

"Let me show you," said Kit.

Kit then pulled out the map and studied it until he found what he was looking for. Then he motioned for Roberto to sit next to him as he placed the folded map on his knee.

Once Roberto was properly situated, Kit put his finger on the map. "We are here," he said.

Then he pointed to a spot on the current trail, but about two inches southwest of the first spot on the map.

"We need to get from here to here," said Kit, as he moved his finger from their current position on the trail to a point south-west of them to a second point on the trail.

Roberto followed his finger and nodded his head he understood.

"This allows us to get around the area where the cops are and would allow us to return to the trail and make our way to our destination of Polebridge," said Kit.

"That doesn't look so hard," said Roberto.

Kit laughed. "That's because it's just two inches on the map. In reality, it's about eight miles over very rough terrain and that includes crossing the continental divide at about nine thousand feet above sea level. Not only will it be difficult, but remember we have a very unhappy companion we have to bring with us," he said.

"Oh," said Roberto. It was obvious to Kit he was not liking what he was hearing. He looked like someone had just punched him in the gut.

After a minute of staring at the map, Roberto looked up with a question in his eyes.

"How do we do this?" he asked.

"That's a damn good question," replied Kit. "The only way I can think of is we search for a game trail that heads in the general direction we want to go."

"General direction?" asked Roberto.

"Animals do not always go from point A to Point B in a straight line or the shortest route," replied Kit. "We may have to keep looking for trails and jumping from one to another."

"How do we do that?" asked a puzzled looking Roberto.

"We use our eyes and this little device," said Kit as he pulled out what looked like a cell phone from his pack.

"What the hell is that?" asked Roberto.

"That, my friend, is a Garmin satellite map," responded a smiling Kit.

"Satellite map? How does it work?" asked Roberto.

"It operates on batteries," said Kit. "Once I turn it on it will locate three different satellites in the sky and then it will provide an accurate fix to exactly where we are down to a distance of a few yards. As we move it will show us exactly where we are relative to the map."

Roberto still looked confused, so Kit added a bit to his explanation. "We are going to have to follow the terrain and that means we may be zig zagging and even back tracking as we try to make our way to our objective on the trail. The

Garmin keeps us aware of where we are and allows us to keep trying to maintain the heading we originally started out on," he said.

"I get it," said Roberto, but both the look on his face and the tone of his voice said he really wasn't sure if he did.

Kit stood up and shouldered his pack. Then he carefully scanned the area where they had been resting. His eyes moved in a half circle and then stopped. He pointed to a point past where their prisoner sat, his back against a pine tree.

"See that opening in the brush about twenty yards behind the tree where Gonzalez is sitting?" asked Kit.

Robert looked where kit was pointing and then he said, "Yes, I see it."

"That, my friend, is a game trail and it looks to be headed southwest and southwest is where we want to be headed," said Kit. "Let's saddle up and see where this thing takes us."

Kit led the way, with Roberto behind him and a reluctant Gonzalez bringing up the rear. Gonzalez was reluctantly obedient, as he had figured out that an encounter with the local vengeful local cops was likely to get him killed.

Chapter Twenty-Three

The game trail was narrow and subject to frequent turns and twists. A straight line on the trail was usually no more than five or ten yards. Kit noticed the trail moved to the south-west, effectively taking them further away from the main trail.

The trail was one twist and turn after another. Occasionally other, smaller trails broke off from the main game trail and more than once, Kit had to try to decide which branch to follow. He kept his eye on the Garmin on his belt and always chose the path that continued toward the southwest.

After almost two and a half hours, Kit came out of a thicket of aspen trees and found himself looking out over a glacier. He checked the map. He was staring at Thunderbird glacier. The glacier rested at the foot of Thunderbird Mountain. According to the map the mountain crested at about eight thousand seven hundred feet above sea level. From where Kit was standing, the mountain looked to rise about fifteen hundred feet above the glacier.

Kit made his way down the game path moving toward the glacier. He could see what looked like pools of water on the south side of the glacier. Those would be a good source of water for them. The sun was going to set in less than two hours. He decided they would make camp there for the night.

It actually took almost two hours to reach the south-east edge of the glacier. Once they were next to a pool of water, Kit hurried to gather firewood and left Roberto to keep an eye on their prisoner. Kit managed to build a small fire pit and stacked his wood supply next to it. He didn't have to go far to find wood. There were several smaller dead pine trees within fifty yards of the fire pit. Once he had the fire going, Kit built a small lean to of small logs on the north side of the fire. Usually, he built a reflector fire to reflect heat to where he would place a sleeping bag. In this case he wanted the lean-to in place to shield the light from anyone looking their way from the north where the main trail was located.

While Kit was building his small lean-to, Roberto sat by the fire, slowly feeding it wood. His job was to keep the fire going, not to make it bigger. Once Kit had the wooden lean-to done, he dug up dirt and covered the wooden platform with about three inches of dirt. The dirt helped shield the light and it added to the insulation of the wood to reflect heat back where Kit wanted it.

When Kit finished the reflector lean-to, it was dark. He used the light from the fire to heat some water. Then he took three packs of chili from his pack. He cut off the tops of the foil packets and set them next to the fire. When the water was starting to boil on the fire, he took the small pot off the fire and poured hot water into each foil packet. Then he used a small wooden spoon to stir the contents of each packet until the water was absorbed.

Kit used his combination folding knife and travel spoon/fork and sampled the result from one of the packets. He reached in his pack and took out a small plastic container of salt and sprinkled a bit on top of each packet. Then he stirred each packet with the wooden spoon. He tried a second bite and decided it was fine.

"'Come and get it," said Kit.

Roberto came and took one packet and gave it to Gonzalez alone with a plastic spoon. Then he returned to the fire and took the second packet. For the next few minutes there was no noise in the air except for the crackling of the wood burning on the small fire.

Kit made some instant coffee and handed a cup to Roberto. Both men drank their coffee in silence as they stared into the flames of the small wood fire.

"How far are we from the trail?" said Roberto finally.

Kit thought for a second and then said, "From the original trail I have no idea. But, from the point on the trail I am trying to reach I would venture a guess of at least five or six miles," he said.

"How long should it take us to reach that point on the trail?" asked Roberto.

"I have no idea what the terrain will be like, so my best guess is three to six hours," replied Kit.

"When we reach the trail again, how far will we be from this Polebridge place?" asked Roberto.

"If I remember correctly, a bit over seven miles," replied Kit.

"That seems so far," said Roberto.

"It's really not so far," said Kit. "The trail will be a lot faster than us chasing our tails out here trying to find the best game trail," said Kit. "Once we get back on the main trail, we should make good time."

"God, I hope so," said a weary Roberto.

"You go check on our prisoner, and I'll clean up our supper crap," said Kit.

Roberto got to his feet and by the time he returned to the fire, Kit was fast asleep. A weary Roberto joined him in a deep slumber within a matter of a few minutes.

Chapter Twenty-Four

Kit was up a daybreak. He got the small fire restarted and put water on to boil. Roberto awoke and went to take Gonzalez for a bathroom break back in the rocks. Each man got a hot cup of instant coffee and some crackers for breakfast. They quickly cleaned up their gear, doused the fire with plenty of dirt, then stamping the dirt down with their boots. Then they resumed their hike on the best-looking game trail they could find heading at least somewhat southwest.

Two hours later Kit signaled for a break. They had spent too much time and energy going up and down, back and forth, and seemingly making little progress. They were about a quarter way up what appeared by to a rugged pass cutting through Thunderbird Mountain, and he halted them under a cluster of twisted pine trees. They got a little shade and a break from the constant wind.

Kit and Roberto dropped their packs and the three men sprawled on the loose rocks under the trees. Kit was winded. The climb had been difficult and full of twists and turns. He looked over at Roberto. He looked exhausted, and their prisoner didn't look any better.

Kit took out a water bottle and took a big swig of water. He knew it was important to keep hydrated, especially at altitude. He glanced over at his two sprawled companions.

They were still breathing hard. That wasn't good. Then he looked around and up from their current position.

He could see nothing that looked remotely like any civilized person had ever been on this trail. Kit got to his feet and then retrieved his small binoculars from his shirt pocket. He brought them up and began to try to scan the trail above them and the area around it. He saw no movement save branches of occasional pine trees waving in the strong mountain winds.

He was about to put the binoculars away when he caught a flash of blue on the trail above him. Nature didn't have many animals or birds colored blue and certainly not anything that big. He focused the binoculars, and then he was able to locate the elusive blue patch again.

The blue was a ball cap. The cap was on a man. The man was moving slowly in their direction. As the man drew closer, Kit was able to make out more details. He was just under six feet in height. He appeared to be in his late twenties or early thirties. He was white, and he had a scraggly brown beard. He moved easily and smoothly like a man who was extremely comfortable in nature. He had tan pants, a camo shirt, hiking boots, and a large, but seemingly empty pack on his back.

Kit put the binoculars back in his pocket. Then he turned to Roberto and tapped him on the shoulder to get his attention.

"I'm going to scout again a bit," he whispered to Roberto. "I thought I saw something, and I'm going to check it out."

Roberto was breathing normally now, and he looked up at Kit in confusion. "What do you see?" he asked.

"Not sure," replied Kit. "I'll be back in a few minutes. Stay put and stay quiet."

Roberto nodded his head in agreement. Kit moved quietly and slipped out from under the sheltering pine trees. He moved slowly and carefully. He kept his eye on the blue cap and moved toward the man, but at an angle to his right so he would not be seen until he wanted to be seen.

Each time Kit moved, he paused and remained motionless for a bit as he surveyed the area around him. By now he was close enough to notice that while the man appeared watchful, he was spending most of his time studying the ground in front of and around him, seldom looking up.

Kit decided he must be looking for something, but what? It took Kit about twenty minutes to move slowly and quietly to where he was now on the man's left flank and was up the slope about twenty feet higher than the man was.

The man continued to slowly come down the slope, pausing every few feet. Kit slipped his expandable baton out of its small holster and then decided to announce himself. Kit rose from behind a scraggly bush directly to the man's right and said, "Howdy."

The man jumped like he'd just stepped in a patch of rattlesnakes. He was clearly surprised to discover anything, let alone a man, that close to him.

Kit stood there, not moving, but smiling, with his hands at his side, including his right hand which held the expandable baton.

Kit could see the man's features much more clearly at this distance, and he was likely in his early thirties. He was lean and looked hard muscled. He saw surprise and just a touch of fear in the man's eyes.

"Who the hell are you?" asked the man.

"My name is Carson Andrews, but my friends call me Kit," he replied.

"Kit? You mean like in Kit Carson, the old Indian scout?" replied the man.

"Yup," said Kit. "One and the same. And you are?"

"Jake. Jake McKusker," replied the man, his body seemingly slightly relaxed as he let tension drain out of him.

"Well, Jake McKusker, what the hell are you doing poking around up here in the middle of a national park?" asked Kit. He had learned to ask questions early. It kept the other guy a bit off balance, as he searched for an answer when he should have been focused on Kit.

"Maybe I should ask you the same question," said Jake. "This ain't no public trail and the rangers hereabouts don't take kindly to folks wanderin' around in places they probably shouldn't be."

"I doubt we run into any rangers up here," said Kit with a disarming smile. "They got their hands full with stupid, overweight tourists getting in all sorts of trouble on the one paved road in the park."

Jake laughed. "You got that right," he said. Then he took a more serious turn. "What are you doin' up here?" he asked.

"It's a long story and my mouth is kinda dry from stayin' quiet while I tried to flank you up here," replied Kit. "How about we walk down to that little grove of pine trees and discuss it. My party's resting there."

"Your party?" asked Jake. "How many more of you are there?"

"Just one of me," said Kit. "I'm a guide and was hired to take a party through the park. There's two of them. One hired me and the other is a killer we captured in the park."

"Killer? In the park? Are you pullin' my leg?" asked Jake.

"I tell you what. Let's walk down there and get settled and have a drink of water, and I'll do my best to explain what I think is going on here," said Kit.

"Lead the way," said Jake.

Kit headed back down the slope with Jake right behind him. When they reached the grove of pine trees, Kit dropped his pack and found a rock to sit on. Jake took a rock a few feet away, but kept his oversized, but empty looking pack on his back.

Roberto got to his feet and Kit introduced him. "This here is Roberto. He's my client for this goat roping screw up. The other gent is a cartel killer named Gonzalez. We captured him on the trail a ways back. I been paid to find him, capture him, and return him and Roberto to his boss just outside the park," said Kit.

Jake took off his cap and ran his hand through his hair. Then he put his cap back on. "You sure you ain't been out in the sun too long, or maybe been smoking some kind of loco weed. I've heard a lot of crazy shit in my time, but mister, that story of yours probably takes first prize for the wacko award," said Jake.

Kit reached in his pack and grabbed a water bottle and took a long drink. Then he replaced the bottle and faced Jake.

"I told you it was a long and goofy story," said Kit. Then he smiled and proceeded to tell the story of how he got involved and why he was currently stuck on a game trail in the middle of nowhere in Glacier National Park.

When he was finished, Jake looked at him like he was a bug under a microscope. "That's probably the most bullshit story I ever heard," he said.

"Maybe so, but everything I told you is true," said Kit.

Jake grabbed his own water bottle and took a big swig. Then he looked over at Roberto and then Gonzalez, as though he was making sure they were flesh and blood and not some sort of mirage.

"I've been honest with you, Jake," said Kit. "Now maybe you can tell me what you're doing up here in the middle of nowhere, all by yourself, scanning the ground around you as you walked, like you were looking for gold nuggets."

Jake smiled and then he shrugged off his pack. He opened the top of the pack and extracted a good-sized deer antler. "I'm an antler rustler," said Jake with a big grin.

"Antler rustler? What the hell is that?" asked Kit.

"Deer, elk, and moose all shed their antlers every year and grow new ones," said Jake. "I come in the park and go off trail and look for them. When I find them, I stick them in my backpack."

"Why?" asked Kit.

"Why do I collect antlers?" asked Jake. "Where you from? You sure as hell ain't from Montana."

"I'm from Wyoming," replied Kit with a grin.

"Then you should know why I'm collectin' antlers. They sell for big bucks to dealers from China and places in the Far East where they use them for God knows what," said Jake.

"So, why are you an antler rustler?" asked Kit.

Jake paused and looked hard at Kit. "You sure you're from Wyoming?" he asked.

"Sure am," replied Kit. "I live in Kemmerer. Ever been there?"

"Kemmerer? No, can't say I ever heard of it," answered Jake.

"Can't say I'm surprised," said a smiling Kit. "But you haven't answered my question. Why are you an antler rustler?"

"It's a sideline for me," said Jake. "I'm an electrician and have a small shop just outside of Whitefish. I started in huntin' for antlers about ten years ago. I soon figured out that lots of folks go roamin' around in the woods looking for antlers. Lots of competition. Then I figured out that it was illegal to take antlers or anything else out of a national park. I took a couple of hikes into the park and found lots of antlers. Been at it ever since."

"You found lots of antlers?" asked Kit.

"I sure did, and even today, after ten years of collectin' them, I still find plenty," said Jake.

"So, nobody stops you? Nobody checks your pack or questions why you're taking antlers out of the park?" asked Kit.

"They would if they saw me, but they never have," said a smiling Jake.

"You sneak into the park and collect antlers and then sneak out with them?" asked Kit.

"Cause it's illegal to collect them and take them out of the park," said Jake with a look on his face that said he couldn't believe how naïve Kit must be. "If you get caught," he added.

"And you don't get caught?" asked Kit. "Let me get this straight, you sneak into the park; collect all the antlers you can find and then sneak out of the park and sell them to some Chinese brokers for cash."

"Bingo. Give the guy a cigar," said Jake derisively.

"How do you manage to avoid getting caught?" asked Kit.

"I grew up hunting and fishing," said Jake. "I know my way around the park after ten years of exploring it. Most of the rangers in the park never get out of their offices or their trucks. I rarely run into one of them boys out on a trail. And when I do, I can hear them comin' from half a mile away. It's easy to avoid them."

Kit paused and took another drink of water. When he put his water bottle down, he had come up with an idea.

"Can I ask how much you make in a year poaching antlers in the park?" said Kit

"You can ask, but that's my business, not yours," replied Jake curtly.

"I'm assuming your antler sideline is because being an electrician in Whitefish doesn't pay all that well," said Kit.

"Yes and no," replied Jake. "My business pays pretty well, but the damn government has their hand out for taxes, licenses, permits, and all kinds of crap, not to mention insurance and utilities. My antler sideline lets me have extra cash and avoid all that other nonsense." Then Jake smiled. "Besides, I like being outdoors in the mountains and I enjoy huntin' for antlers as much as I enjoy huntin' for game."

"Would you be interested in doing a little guide business for cash. No questions asked?" inquired Kit.

"You got my attention, Mr. Andrews," said Jake.

"It's Kit, not Mr. Andrews. Don't make me feel older than I am," said Kit with a grin.

"What kind of guidin' are we talking about?" asked Jake.

"The kind you do, get paid, and then forget it ever happened," replied Kit.

"Sounds like my kind of job," replied Jake. "Explain the job."

Kit got out his map and unfolded part of it that showed their current position and the trail to Polebridge. He put the map on his knees and Jake moved over and sat next to him. Kit pointed to their current position.

"We're here," he said. "And this is where I want to rejoin the trail to Polebridge," as he moved his finger on the map. "Can you get us there and if so, how long will it take?"

Jake studied the map for a second and then looked up and smiled. "Not a problem," he said. He looked at his watch. "I can get you to Polebridge by about four o'clock tomorrow afternoon, more or less."

"What's more or less mean?" asked a suspicious Kit.

"It means unless we get slowed down by weather or other folks lookin' for that jasper," said Jake pointing to Gonzalez.

"How much?" asked Kit.

Jake stroked his chin and then looked up at Kit. "A thousand bucks," he said.

"Let's make it five thousand," said Kit.

When Jake looked surprised, Kit smiled. "I want it done right," he said.

"You got it," said Jake. The two men shook hands, and both got to their feet.

"Let's go," said Kit. "We're moving out."

Chapter Twenty-Five

The little column set out on the game trail with Jake in the lead, followed by Kit, and then Gonzalez with Roberto trailing him. Jake led them up to the small knoll where Kit had first seen him, and he followed the game trail for about half a mile.

When they reached a spot on the game trail where it veered to the left at a large boulder with a split on one side, Jake executed a sudden turn to the right through two large sagebrush plants. Kit noted his surprise at the actual room between the two sagebrush when it looked like there was none.

On the other side of the two sagebrush, there was another game trail. This one was more well-worn and a bit wider than the old one. Jake led the way as the trail wound back and forth as they climbed higher up the side of the mountain. Kit recognized the use of switch backs by the animals, just like a human engineer would do.

They stopped to rest about every two hours. Kit was sure Jake didn't need the break, but now he was keeping close tabs on Roberto and Gonzalez, neither of whom was in particularly good physical shape.

Each time they stopped Jake directed them to take a drink of water. He cautioned them to drink slowly and not to drink too much. After a break of ten minutes, Jake would stand up and get them on their way again.

The climbing was hard, and everyone was breathing deeply. Occasionally either Roberto or Gonzalez would involuntarily halt, and the rest would have to do the same. When that happened, Jake would allow only a three-minute rest and then he would order them to move on.

They had been walking for a little over five hours when they reached a narrow ravine that was hidden until they were right on top of it. The path led down into the ravine and Jake headed down into it. He moved slowly and carefully and was quickly at the bottom. Then he stopped and turned to watch the rest of the small party make their way carefully to the spot he was standing on.

Kit could see the ravine was a form of shortcut that led to the other side of the mountain without having to go all the way to the top and then all the way down. Within twenty minutes they were on the other side of the mountain.

Jake halted them there and directed them to rest. They all took water, and Jake reached into his pack and grabbed a small plastic bag. He opened it and passed it back to Kit. In the bag were strips of homemade jerky. Kit took a piece and passed the bag to Roberto, who took out two pieces and gave one to Gonzalez. They sat on boulders, chewed on their jerky, and drank water. Kit made a note to himself to remember jerky when he went out in the wilderness in the future.

"What is it?" asked Kit.

Jake grinned. "Guess," he said.

Kit chewed on his for a bit and said, "It's not beef."

"Nope," said Jake. "It's elk."

"You hunt?" asked Kit.

"Whenever I can," replied Jake.

"You make this?" asked Kit.

"Yup," said Jake. "Learned from my old man."

"Good recipe," said Kit.

"Family secret," said Jake with a smile.

"Not surprised," said Kit.

Jake looked at his watch. "Time to move out," he said as he got to his feet.

Kit and the others rose to their feet and Jake again led the way on the trail, but now the trail was trending downward and with less switchbacks.

After an hour of walking Kit noticed they were making better time. He glanced up at the sun. It was sinking further to the west. He guessed they had about two hours of daylight left at best.

"How much further?" he asked

Jake looked up at the sun and then back at Kit. "In about an hour we'll be about a mile from the park trail. We'll stop at a spot with a small spring and spend the night. We'll be close to the trail, but far enough from it not to get seen," he said.

Kit nodded his head in agreement. In about forty minutes Jake put up his hand as a silent signal to stop. He moved back beside Kit.

"We're almost there. I'll go ahead and scout out the site. I'll be back in fifteen minutes or less," said Jake.

Kit motioned for Roberto and Gonzalez to take a seat, and Jake disappeared from their view.

Chapter Twenty-Six

Jake was back in ten minutes. He appeared suddenly from behind a large sagebrush. Kit was amazed he had heard nothing to indicate Jake's approach. He stopped next to Kit.

"Everything all right?" asked Kit.

"All clear," replied Jake. He looked over where Roberto and Gonzalez sat. "Git them boys on their feet and let's move out. We ain't got a lot of daylight left."

"You heard the man," said Kit. "On your feet. We're heading for a campsite."

Roberto and Gonzalez got awkwardly to their feet. They were sore and stiff from the long hike and the faster pace Jake had set. But the idea of a campsite, food, and rest seeped into their tired brains, and they were more than ready to move.

Jake led the way and within five minutes they were at the site. The site Jake had picked had a small grove of pine trees nestled up against a sheer stone wall that rose over fifteen feet. At the base of the trees was a small spring and a small pool of water that sat in a bed of rocks. The pool was cold and the water clear.

Jake grabbed his water bottles and so did Kit. They quickly refilled their bottles. Roberto and Gonzalez collapsed on the ground, grateful for the shade and the sheltered spot out of the constant wind.

Jake and Kit set about arranging sleeping positions and pulling out the gear they would need from their packs. Roberto and Gonzalez reluctantly and slowly followed suit. Kit used his boots to kick out a clear spot for a fire, but then Jake put his hand on Kit's arm.

"No fire," said Jake. "Even if the flame is small, the smoke can give our position away. This needs to be a cold camp."

"Maybe not," said Kit with a smile. He reached in his pack and drew out his tiny stove. He showed it to Jake and then showed him the foil packets of food.

"It burns leaves and twigs and there is hardly any smoke," said Kit. "It heats water and when it boils, I pour hot water into the packets and stir. Instant supper."

"Cool," said Jake.

"The only thing is I'm almost out of foil packets, so we eat what I find," said Kit.

"What have you got?" asked Jake as he eyed the foil packets.

"Let's see," said Kit. "I've got two packets of chili, one of spaghetti, and one of corned beef hash."

"Ain't a loser in the bunch," said Jake. "I thought those foil packets had crap like tofu, sprouts, and junk like that."

"Maybe some do, but not the stuff I buy," said a smiling Kit.

Kit pulled down the legs on the tiny stove and set it up while Jake scouted the ground for twigs and leaves. Kit set the fuel into the tiny chamber in the stove and lit it with a farmer's match. Jake fed the small fire while Kit put water in the kettle and then set it on top of the little stove.

Kit and Jake sat cross-legged by the stove waiting for the water to boil. Jake fed the fire while Kit grabbed the four foil packets and cut open the tops. Then he set the opened packets up against a nearby rock.

When the water came to a boil, Kit had Jake hold the packets while Kit carefully poured boiling water into each foil packet. Then he used his spoon/fork combination to stir the contents. When he was done, he randomly handed a packet to Jake, Roberto, and Gonzalez, leaving the last packet for himself. Each man had his own spoon, except Gonzalez and Roberto handed him his spare spoon.

There was absolute silence except for the sounds of men eating and slurping down their hot meal. When they were finished, Kit collected the packets and buried them behind some rocks. The men cleaned up their spoons and put them in their pockets, except for Gonzalez. He wasn't allowed to have anything he might be able to use, and Roberto collected his spoon.

It was almost dark. Kit left the tiny stove out to cool off and then slid into his sleeping bag. Soon the campsite was silent except for the occasional sound of someone snoring. Jake took the first two-hour watch. He and Kit had agreed between themselves they would alternate guard duty to insure they didn't get surprised during the night. Jake had reluctantly agreed after making it clear to Kit that the only possible nighttime visitors to their camp would likely be animals or birds. The park rangers he knew were too lazy or unsure of themselves to go prowling around the park in the dead of night.

Kit was awakened at dawn by a nudge from Jake. He sat up in the dim light. He was suddenly alert and quickly scanned his surroundings for a possible threat.

"Relax," said Jake in a quiet voice. "Ain't nobody awake or movin' except the two of us."

Then Jake handed him a cup of hot coffee. "I used your little stove. I had two packets of decent instant coffee left and used them. Your stove will be cool by the time we head out."

Kit gratefully accepted the metal cup of hot coffee. He sipped it and then looked over at Jake. "This isn't half bad. It's a lot better than my instant coffee."

"It's ok, but it's still crap compared to real coffee," said Jake as he sipped his coffee.

Kit took another sip and then stared at his cup. "Who makes this coffee?" he asked.

"I got no idea," said Jake. "I bought some from a customer who raved about it. Come to think about it, I think this might have been my last two packs."

Kit looked around and found one of the two empty packets Jake had used. He stuffed the packet into his pocket.

"I'll check it out later," said Kit. "If I can find it, I'll send you a box."

"Deal," said a smiling Jake.

"How close to the trail are we?" asked Kit.

"About a mile and a half," replied Jake. "We should hit the trail in a little over an hour, depending on the pace we can keep those two yahoos at."

"Are you planning on making any breakfast?" asked Jake.

"I hadn't planned on it," said Kit.

Jake leaned over and dug into his pack. "How about we use these?" he said.

Kit looked at him. He was holding four energy bars. "Those and water should be fine," said Kit.

The men finished their coffee and then washed out their cups and packed them and the small stove away.

Kit woke up Roberto and Gonzalez and soon they were packed up and ready to hit the trail. Kit gave each of them an energy bar and a water bottle. "The walking should be easy," he said. "Eat and drink while we walk."

Jake took the lead and the tiny column of hikers set out to the southwest. Kit looked up at the early morning sky. Except for a few scattered clouds, the sky was as blue as the ocean.

Chapter Twenty-Seven

Jake had been correct. In just under an hour, he raised his right arm in a signal to stop. Then he motioned to Kit to join him. Kit turned and looked directly at Roberto and Gonzalez. He put his finger to his lips to indicate they needed to remain silent and then carefully made his way up to where Jake was kneeling in some high grass.

When he knelt next to Jake, Kit immediately began to take in the surrounding view. Jake pointed to an opening in the brush in front of them. Through that opening, Kit could see the main trail. He reached in his pocket and drew out his small binoculars. Kit placed them over his eyes, made a minor adjustment on the binoculars and then scanned the trail. Then he handed them to Jake who also scanned the trail and the area around it. Then he returned them to Kit, who replaced them in his shirt pocket.

After a nod from Jake, Kit turned and used an arm signal to direct Roberto and Gonzalez to join them. In a couple of minutes, the four men were kneeling close together in the high grass. Jake spoke briefly in a whisper.

"Follow right behind me. Make no noise. If I put my arm up, stop where you are. Understood?" he said.

Kit, Roberto, and even Gonzalez nodded their heads that they understood. With that settled, Jake rose to a crouch and slowly made his way down the faint game trail toward the main park trail.

After quite a bit of zigging and zagging, Kit stepped over a dead log on the game trail. When he stepped past it, he found himself almost running into Jake's back. Jake was standing still and studying his surroundings. Kit needed no urging to do likewise. Neither man saw anything unusual nor threatening.

In front of them was the park trail that led to Polebridge, their destination. Jake turned to face Kit and stuck out his hand. Kit smiled and shook it.

"You weren't kidding when you said you knew your way around this park," said Kit.

"I been hiking through this park for ten years," replied a smiling Jake. "It's like walking through my back yard for me."

"If you give me your mailing address, I'll be damn sure to get you the $5,000 I promised you for getting us here," said Kit.

"I agreed to $1,000," replied Jake. "I don't consider this job done until I get you out of this damn park, and we ain't there yet. I'll give you the address when we are standin' on Montana land, not a national park owned by the damned feds."

"You have a deal," said Kit. "What do you suggest for the rest of this forced march?"

"I think we keep the same plan we used to get here," said Jake. "I lead and do the scoutin' and you follow with your two-legged cargo."

"You lead, I'll follow," said Kit.

Jake stepped out on the trail and took a few steps forward. Then he stopped, listened, and looked around him. When he was satisfied that they were completely alone, He motioned to Kit and began striding southwest on the trail.

Kit motioned to Roberto to follow him. Roberto prodded Gonzalez, and they followed about five yards behind Kit. They moved slowly to maintain as much silence as possible. That was helpful to Roberto and Gonzalez who were pushing the end of their rope physically. Both men were unaccustomed to hard continuous hiking, especially when it included hiking up and down steep inclines.

After an hour and a half, Jake raised his hand up and the little column halted. "Let's get off the trail and take a break," said Jake softly.

The four men slipped off the trail and disappeared into the surrounding brush. There were few large trees on the side of the trail, but there was a lot of chest high heavy brush. Jake led them into a tiny clearing in the brush. Once there they sat on rocks, stumps, the ground, or whatever was handy. Roberto and Gonzalez were breathing hard. Kit decided Jake had noticed or heard their heavy breathing and decided a rest was in order.

Kit sat next to Jake. He pulled a water bottle out of his pack and took a drink. Then he offered it to Jake who took the bottle and managed a long swig of water. He returned the bottle, and Kit slipped it back into his pack.

"How far do you think we are from Polebridge?" asked Kit softly.

Jake did not immediately respond. Kit could tell he was trying to do an estimate from memory. Finally, he seemed to be satisfied with his thought and he spoke.

"My best guess is somewhere between twelve and fifteen miles. That's the bad news. The good news is the trail is mostly level or downhill. We should be able to average about 2 to 3 miles an hour, depending on how well your two companions can hold up. From what I've seen so far, they ain't up to being outdoors much, and they sure as hell ain't up to hiking in the mountains. I'll be damned surprised if we don't have to carry that Gonzalez cat the last mile or so."

Kit laughed. "If he can't make it, we'll put a rope around him and drag his ass the last mile," said Kit.

Jake joined in the soft laughter. "That I'd pay money to see." Jake looked at his watch. "We've been sitting on our asses long enough," he said. He rose to his feet. "I'll check the trail to make sure it's clear. You wait here until I return."

"Will do," replied Kit.

Jake stepped past a large bush and disappeared. A few minutes later he reappeared and motioned for Kit and the others to follow him. Soon they were at the edge of the trail.

Jake stepped out and after listening and looking both ways, He motioned for the others to follow him.

They walked for another hour and other than the songs of birds and the occasional rabbit or squirrel scurrying across the trail they saw or heard nothing. Kit had gotten used to watching Jake's back, and he kept about a fifteen-yard distance between him and his scout.

Suddenly Jake came to a halt. Kit could see something had alerted him. Kit looked and listened, and he could neither see nor hear anything. Then he heard it.

Kit had never served in the military like his half-brother or Swifty, but he had heard the thump, thump, thump of a helicopter more than once since he had moved to Wyoming.

"Get off the trail and get down under cover," yelled Jake.

The four men ran off the trail and into the nearest cover. Jake led them to a grove of Aspen trees that was situated about twenty yards north of the trail. Jake and Kit grabbed Roberto and Gonzalez and literally tossed them into bushes located under the trees.

None of the four men made a sound as the helicopter passed slowly over the trail and where they had been standing just seconds before. All Kit could hear was the sound of the helicopter, its rotors beating hard and the downdraft moving the limbs of the trees around them. After a bit, the sounds began to fade. Then all Kit could hear was the heavy breathing of tired men who had just had the crap scared out of them.

Kit rose to his knees and scanned his surroundings. He could see nothing. He listened. Even the birds were silent. They had been disturbed by the helicopter just as the four men had. It was unexpected and unwelcome.

Jake appeared next to Kit. He too was looking and listening. After a few minutes he spoke.

"Looked to me like they was looking for someone," he said.

"I bet you're right," replied Kit.

"They were flying too low and slow for just moving over the park," said Jake. "I can't remember the last time I've ever seen or heard a helicopter while I've been in this park."

"Killing two cops provides a lot of motivation for law enforcement to pull out all the stops," said Kit.

"From what you said, the cops must have caught the cartel boys and their helpers, but they know they're lookin' for Gonzalez and they gotta know he's the killer of those two prison cops," said Jake.

"I think we have to assume we're gonna get a full court press from the cops until they capture or kill our unwelcome companion," said Kit.

Jake put his finger to his lips in front of Kit. Then he rose to his feet and slipped into the underbrush. Kit remained on his knees and motioned for Roberto and Gonzalez to remain where they were and to keep quiet.

Jake reappeared and knelt next to Kit.

"I didn't hear or see anything on the trail. I think we can resume our hike," he said.

"Anything else?" asked Kit.

"Yeah. I'm starting to think this gig is a $5,000 job, not the $1,000 job I originally thought," said Jake with a sly smile.

"$5,000 it is," replied a grinning Kit. "Let's just get the hell out of this park."

Jake rose to his feet, followed by Kit. Kit motioned to Roberto, and he and Gonzalez soon joined them. Jake led the way back to the trail. Ten minutes later, the four men were slowly making their way southwest on the park trail.

Chapter Twenty-Eight

The small column of four male hikers continued on the trail for another hour. The birds had returned, but they saw no small mammals. The trail was mostly level and when it did change, it usually sloped slightly downhill.

After an hour of hiking, Jake called a halt. The small party stepped off the trail and moved into a rocky area where large boulders formed almost a wall between the four men and the trail. They flopped down behind the rocks and tried to rest. Kit produced his water bottles, and Jake magically produced four energy bars. The men wolfed down the energy bars, and each took several long drinks of water.

Kit sat on a rock next to Jake. "When we get out of here, them two boys will sleep for a week," said Jake.

"I'll be right with them," said Kit. "Any idea how much farther?" he asked.

"I'm pretty damn sure we're almost to the north end of Bowman Lake. I recollect there's a shelter near that end of the lake," said Jake. "If I remember correctly, it's about ten miles from the shelter to the trail head at Polebridge."

"How's the trail?" asked Kit.

"Pretty level and gentle," replied Jake.

"Do we stop and rest at the shelter?" asked Kit.

"We can, but I'd hate to get caught flatfooted in that shelter and have a slew of cops show up," said Jake. "That would make me very uncomfortable."

"We'd both be uncomfortable, but that'd be small change to how Gonzalez would feel," said Kit.

Both men looked at each other and laughed.

The men waited for about fifteen minutes when Jake suddenly threw up his hand as a silent signal to halt. Everyone literally froze in the position they were in. Jake motioned for them to get down, and they did. They he crept forward and disappeared around a sharp bend in the trail. Kit went to one knee and waited. He looked and listened but could detect nothing that alarmed him.

Jake quickly appeared around the sharp bend in the trail. He moved next to Kit and went to one knee.

"What's up?' asked Kit softly.

"The shelter and the start of the lake are just ahead," said Jake. "I counted about half a dozen hikers resting at the shelter. We need to get off the trail and lay low until they move on."

Kit nodded his head in agreement and then made a hand signal to Roberto to keep quiet and follow his lead. Roberto nodded his head that he understood.

Jake led them to the north or upside of the trail and led them through a thicket of bushes with sharp thorns. Once he had led the group off the trail to a spot about thirty yards uphill, he put his hand up as a signal to stop. Jake had led them to a tiny hole in the thicket that was just big enough for the four men.

Everyone dropped their packs and tried to find a comfortable spot to sit. Kit whispered to Roberto to let him know why they had stopped and exited the trail.

Gonzalez asked no questions. He knew he would never get an answer anyway. His only interest was in staying alive.

The foursome sat in silence for almost twenty minutes. Finally, Jake stood up. He stood absolutely still, as his eyes and ears tried to pick up any movement or sounds. Then he motioned for the rest of the group to stand.

"They're gone," he whispered. "Grab your packs and follow me back to the trail."

Packs were grabbed and slipped on, and Jake led them back to the trail. There he had them wait about five yards off the trail. He stepped on the trail and after checking for sound or movement, he motioned for the other three men to join him.

Kit caught up to Jake and whispered, "Which way did they go?"

Jake looked at him and grinned. "They went southwest, headed to Polebridge. We'll follow them all the way there. They will act as an early warning system for anyone else coming up the trail from Polebridge."

Kit nodded and dropped back behind Jake. He soon had adjusted his position where he was fifteen yards in Jake's rear. Roberto and Gonzalez were about the same distance behind Kit.

They walked in silence. The only noise coming from the sounds their shoes and boots made as they hit the ground with each stride they took. Kit could hear birds in the trees again and took that as a good sign.

After another hour and a half, Jake called a halt. They slipped off the trail and moved into a small clearing surrounded by young Aspen trees. Jake handed out more energy bars, and everyone washed them down with water from their bottles.

Jake looked over at Kit and grinned. Then he spoke, softly. "The answer to the question you've been thinking about, but haven't asked, is we are about 6 or 7 miles from Polebridge. We have been walking on the north side of Bowman Lake. My guess is we have about four miles to go before we hit the west end of the lake."

"Things are going from bad to worse when you start being able to read my mind," said Kit, shaking his head.

"It was written all over your face," said Jake with a smile.

"I need a new face," said Kit.

Jake laughed. "Ready to head out?" he asked Kit.

"Born ready," replied Kit.

"Let's saddle up. I'll go first and check out the trail," said Jake. He rose to his feet and slipped through the bushes and was gone.

Kit, Roberto, and Gonzalez moved to the edge of the trail and waited. Jake stepped out on the trail and listened and sniffed the air. Satisfied they were alone, he motioned for the rest to join him.

The four hiked slowly along the north side of the lake. They saw more birds and squirrels and surprised two does drinking from the side of the lake. The two deer bounded away into the trees and disappeared.

They were almost to the end of the lake when Jake froze in his tracks. Kit saw him stop and scanned the trail ahead of them to try to detect what had alerted Jake.

"Roberto, grab Gonzalez and get off the trail and get hidden. Now!" said Jake firmly. Then he grabbed Kit by the arm. "Act natural. Act surprised but shut up and let me do the talkin'," said Jake in a serious voice.

Roberto and Gonzalez had disappeared to the north side of the trail and before Kit could ask why, two dogs appeared on the trail, straining on long leases held by two men wearing sheriff's deputy uniforms.

Kit and Jake stood almost like they were frozen in place. The dogs, lean with long droopy ears, were not aggressive, but they quickly tried to sniff both men's pants and boots. They were pulled back by the deputies holding their leashes.

"Sorry," said one of the deputies. "I didn't see you guys on the trail. The dogs won't hurt you, they're just naturally curious." He called to the dog on his leash and the bloodhound came to the deputy's side and sat.

"What's with the dogs?" asked Jake, with as innocent a look on his face as he could manage.

"We have a huge manhunt in the park for a dangerous escaped convict," replied the deputy. "We have a report that several other criminals tried to shoot it out with other law enforcement personnel, and they were captured. They think the escaped convict was in cahoots with this group, but he escaped. We're bringin' up our dogs to pick up his trail and run him to ground."

"Why the hell would an escaped convict try to hide in a national park?" asked an innocent and surprised looking Jake.

"Who knows," replied the deputy. "All I can figure is he thought he could slip through the park and come out in Canada."

"Who were the other bad guys who shot it out with the cops?" asked Jake.

"No idea," said the deputy. "Scuttlebutt on the radio says the convict was a cartel guy and maybe the cartel sent some of their men to help him. Right now, the whole thing is one big confusing mess. You folks stay safe. Get off the trail and out of the park as fast as you can."

"Thank you, officer," said Jake. "We're gettin' the hell out of here as fast as we can."

"Let's go," said the officer to his partner and the two of them and their dogs headed up the trail at a fast clip.

Kit and Jake stood and watched the two officers, and their dogs disappear up the trail.

Kit turned and looked at Jake. "That last statement is probably the only truthful thing you ever said to a cop."

Jake laughed. "Sometimes the truth is the best option."

Jake moved off the trail and returned with Roberto and Gonzalez.

"Let's get movin'," said Jake.

The foursome headed down the trail. They were moving faster than they had all day. It was as if they could smell the end of the trail, a mere three miles away.

Kit could feel it in his bones. He felt the sense of getting close to the end of the journey. As soon as he could pawn off Roberto and Gonzalez to the cartel, he was going back to his hotel room and sleep for two days.

Chapter Twenty-Nine

The last three miles were like a blur to Kit. All he could do was focus on getting to the end of the trail and getting out of the park. Suddenly Kit felt himself bumping into Jake's back. Jake had stopped on the trail.

"What's wrong?" asked a suddenly alert Kit.

"Nothing," replied Jake. "I think we should stop here, and I'll go on ahead and scout out the trail head. We should make sure we don't have some unpleasant surprise waiting for us there. You take these two and settle in off the trail where you are well hidden. I'll be back in a jiffy."

"Works for me," said Kit. He turned and explained the plan to Roberto and the three men slipped off the trail to the south where there was plenty of underbrush to provide cover for them from any prying eyes on the trail.

Kit found an open spot in the brush and the three men flopped down on the ground. Kit was physically spent and compared to Roberto and Gonzalez; he was in great shape. Kit was glad they were close to the end of the trail. He was tired, hungry, and sore.

While they rested, Roberto suddenly came to life. He grabbed at his pack and began to search frantically through the contents.

"What's wrong?" asked a concerned Kit.

"I had forgotten," said Roberto as he continued to dig through the pack. He was tossing things out of the pack and onto the ground next to him.

"Forgotten what?" asked Kit.

"Ah, here it is," said Roberto as he extracted a satellite phone from the pack.

"A satellite phone?" asked Kit.

"Yes," replied Roberto. "My orders were to only use it if I was unable to make contact with the cartel group on the trail. Since they are now prisoners of the Yankee police, I think I need to call in for help."

"Help?" asked Kit.

"Yes," replied Roberto. "When we get to this trailhead, I doubt there will be anyone from the cartel waiting for us. They have no idea where we are and even if we're still alive."

"I thought they would be waiting at the trailhead," said Kit.

"There are not that many cartel men around here," said Roberto. "Of my original group of four, I am the only one left. The group that shot it out with the police in the park numbered three. They had two gringo hired guns with them because they were short-handed."

"So, what are you saying?" asked Kit.

"I'm saying there may not be any cartel men near us, and I need to call to let them know where we are and that we have the package they are looking for. Then they can make arrangements to get us out of here," said a now excited Roberto.

"Does the phone work?" asked Kit.

Roberto held up the phone and pushed the power button. "We shall see in a minute," he replied.

It took a few minutes. Kit could see the phone was searching for three satellites and finally it made a connection. Roberto dialed a number from memory and waited. Finally, he got an answer, and he began speaking in rapid Spanish that Kit was unable to understand. The call lasted about four minutes and then Roberto shut the phone off and slipped it back into his pack.

Kit waited until Roberto had put the phone away. Then he leaned forward and asked in a low voice, "What's the deal?"

Roberto smiled. "It is as I thought," he said. "They have few assets in this area and are bringing in more help. We are to find a place to hide and stay there until tomorrow afternoon when they will have a team to come and rescue us."

The thought of another night in the boonies was not appealing to Kit, but he was not completely surprised at the cartel's manpower problem. He tried to remember how many cartel men he had seen at the cartel's rented house but wasn't sure of the exact number. He thought he had seen a total of seven. Counting the three men killed by the crazed moose and the three captured by the police in the park, plus Roberto, the total number he could account for was seven.

Kit's thoughts were interrupted by the silent arrival of Jake. He kneeled next to Kit and whispered to him. "No cops at the trailhead, but there are two empty police vehicles parked on the road. It's safe to walk out of the park."

"Maybe not," responded Kit. He proceeded to explain to Jake what had occurred during his absence and the details he had about the satellite phone conversation between Roberto and his boss.

"Shit," was Jake's response.

"Could not agree more," said Kit.

"Got a plan?" asked Jake.

"I'm working on one," replied Kit.

"Work faster," said Jake. "The longer we hang out here the greater the odds of someone stumbling on top of us."

Kit smiled at Jake's remark, but he was trying to come up with an interim plan. Then he looked at Jake. "How far are we from your place?" he asked.

Jake put his hands up in response. "Oh, no. You're not getting me involved in harboring some fugitives. I'm fine with guiding you out of the park, but I want no part of housing those two yahoos."

"I'm not talking about harboring anyone," said Kit.

"What then?' asked Jake.

"Are you close enough to your vehicle to go get it and drive back here?" asked Kit.

"Yeah, I am," answered Jake. "it's a bit of a hike, but I could make it in a couple of hours."

"Here's the plan," said Kit. "You hike out of here and go to your vehicle. Then you drive back here and pick us up at a site we agree on now."

"Then what?" asked a concerned Jake.

"You take us to some cheap, fleabag motel and drop us off. I rent us a couple of rooms, and we wait there until Roberto hears from the cartel," said Kit.

Jake looked at Kit like he had grown horns out of his head. Kit could see he was considering the risks.

"O.K." said Jake. "But it's gonna cost you another thousand bucks."

"Deal," said Kit and he extended his hand. Jake shook it and looked over at Roberto and Gonzalez.

"You fill them in after I'm gone. Where do we meet up?" asked Jake.

Kit got out his map and studied it. Then he pointed a finger to a spot on the map. "Right about here," he said. "It's about a mile south of Polebridge and the trailhead. It Looks wooded. I'll cut a slash on a tree close to the road so you can see it."

"I'll be driving a white Ford van with McKusker Electric painted on the side," said Jake. "When I arrive, you get them two in the back of the van, and you slide in the passenger seat. Make it quick when you do. I ain't gonna linger long in one place."

"Sounds like a plan," said a smiling Kit. The two men shook hands, and Jake disappeared back onto the trail.

Kit moved over next to Roberto and Gonzalez and explained they would be hiking out of the park and walking about a mile south on the highway. Then hide and wait for Jake to come and pick them up in his van. Roberto looked relieved. Gonzalez just looked resigned. Kit decided they would rest for another hour and then walk out of the park and south to the pickup site.

Chapter Thirty

The three men made themselves as comfortable as possible and remained hidden in a thicket next to the trail. Over the next hour, Kit heard another group of two or three men heading east on the trail. From the sound of their boots on the trail, he guessed they were likely law enforcement types. Other than that one incident, the trail remained empty and quiet.

Kit checked his watch. When they had remained hidden on the trail for a little over an hour, he whispered to Roberto and Gonzalez it was time to move. The two men slowly rose to their feet. They were tired and stiff. Kit felt a little better, but not much.

He led the way to the edge of the trail. Once there, he halted and stood quietly, looking and listening. He could hear nothing but some birds. Then he saw two squirrels chasing each other from tree to tree. He considered that a good sign and a return to normal on the trail for birds and animals. He motioned for Roberto and Gonzalez to follow him, and he stepped out onto the trail. Again, he paused to look and listen. Hearing nothing out of order, he began to slowly make his way west on the trail.

Minutes passed and Kit felt the pressure as he slowly drew closer to the trailhead. When he got close enough to hear the occasional vehicle passing by on the road bordering the park, he called a silent halt with a raised right hand. Then he motioned to have Roberto and Gonzalez slip off the road and become hidden in the brush.

Kit slipped off the trail and moved slowly and quietly until he was a good fifteen yards off the trail. He slowly made his way parallel to the trail and finally he could see the trailhead through the tall weeds between his location and the trail. The area around the trailhead was empty. He could see two sheriff's vehicles parked on the side of the road. Both vehicles were empty. Kit paused for a couple of minutes and watched and listened as he waited. He could hear nothing. There was no traffic on the road.

He returned to where he had left Roberto and Gonzalez. Before moving out to the trail he addressed them. "Follow me. Do what I do. Do not speak. Do not make any noise. Is that clear?" he asked.

Both Roberto and Gonzalez nodded their heads. Kit checked the plastic ties on Gonzalez's wrists. They were still in place and intact. Satisfied, he got to his feet and motioned for the two men to follow him. At the trail, he again paused to look and listen. Satisfied there was no threat, he led the two men onto the trail, and they hurried at a fast shuffle to the trailhead.

Once there, Kit led them quickly across the blacktop road to the other side. Then he led them into the brush that seemed to constantly border the road. There was some sort of hiking trail that ran parallel to the road and Kit decided to use it as they moved south. As sore and tired as they were, the trio kept up a decent pace and within half an hour they had reached the spot Jake had pointed out to Kit.

Kit moved Roberto and Gonzalez deeper into the brush surrounding the pickup site and then whispered to them to get comfortable. Roberto and Gonzalez grabbed water bottles and greedily drank from them. Kit then handed them his last energy bars, which they wolfed down.

Kit got to his feet and grabbed the energy bar wrappers, stuffing them in a pocket in his pack. Then he carefully made his way out to the edge of the road. After looking and listening for people or vehicles and hearing and seeing none, he stepped out to the road. He unsheathed his knife and found a pine tree close to the road and used the knife to make a slash on the trunk of the tree. Then he stepped back to ensure it would be easily visible from the road. Satisfied, he sheathed his knife and returned to where Roberto and Gonzalez sat hidden from view from the road.

"Now all I have to do is hurry up and wait," thought Kit to himself. He found a comfortable spot and squatted down on the ground where he could lean back against a rock and keep the road in his sight.

Chapter Thirty-One

Time passed slowly for Kit. He remembered how every time he had to wait for something to happen, time seemed to crawl at a snail's pace. He hoped Jake didn't run into any trouble and would show up as soon as possible.

After about thirty minutes Kit could hear snoring coming from both Roberto and Gonzalez. The trip out of the park had taken a toll on both men who were unprepared physically and mentally for what they had endured in the park. Kit forced himself to stay awake. He adjusted his position several times and tried to think of things to take his mind off his sore muscles and tired body. Nothing seemed to work.

His eyelids seemed to gain weight by the minute. His fatigue was winning the battle. Then he heard the sound of an engine, and he blinked his eyes and there before him was Jake in the driver's seat of a white van with the black letters McKusker Electric emblazoned on the side.

Kit pulled himself to his feet and kicked at the feet of his two slumbering companions. "Get up," he loudly whispered. "Get the hell up." A combination of his loud whisper and the blows to their feet brought both Roberto and Gonzalez awake and semi-alert. Both of them staggered to their feet, groping for support where there was none. Kit grabbed them and shoved them in the general direction of the van. When they reached the van, Kit tore open the rear door and shoved each man, one at a time, unceremoniously into the back of the van. Then he slammed the door shut and staggered to the passenger side of the van. He yanked the door open and threw his body into the seat. Before he could reach out to grab the open door, Jake had accelerated back onto the road. The door slammed shut of its own accord.

"Where to?" asked a grinning Jake.

"All the way down to Route 2," said Kit. "There's a motel a bit outside a place called Coram."

"I know Coram," said Jake. "What's the name of this flop house?"

"How do you know it's a flop house?" said an indignant Kit. "Maybe it's the best motel in town."

"Even if it's the best place in Coram, it's a flop house," retorted Jake. Then he laughed. "What's the name of this place?"

Kit pulled out his phone and then waited until it came online. Once it did, he scrolled to a spot and read what he saw. "A motel just out of Coram named the Myrest Motel. It's about 2.4 miles outside of Coram," said Kit.

"Sounds great, if you're a fugitive from justice," laughed Jake.

"Can't be too bad a place," said Kit. "The rooms are $150.00 a night."

"Anything around Glacier National Park is damn expensive," said Jake. "If it's $150 bucks a night, it's probably an old chicken coop."

"Well," said Kit. "At least it ain't high profile."

"High profile? Hell, that place probably has the profile of a dog turd," laughed Jake.

"It's only for one night. It's got to be better than cold, hard, rocky ground," said Kit.

"You keep thinkin' that way," said Jake. "It'll help cushion the shock of what a dump the place really is. At least the mountains ain't infested with roaches."

"How long till we get to Coram?" asked Kit.

"Somewhere around three hours," said Jake.

"Wake me when we get close," said Kit.

"You can count on it," said Jake.

Kit made himself comfortable in the van's passenger seat and within minutes he was fast asleep. He had some turbulent dreams. None of them made any sense and all of them featured him on the run from something. When he awoke, he was sweating like he'd been running hard for a long distance.

"Sleeping Beauty awakens," said Jake sarcastically.

"Where the hell are we?" asked Kit as he rubbed sleep from his eyes and managed to sit upright on his seat.

"We're about fifteen minutes out from Coram," replied Jake.

"Good," responded Kit. As he pushed sleep out of his system, he became aware how stiff his body was from sleeping in a cramped position in the front seat of a commercial van.

"A bit stiff, are we?" asked a smiling Jake.

"I've had boards with more flexibility," responded Kit.

"Better loosen up, we'll be at the motel pretty dang soon," said Jake.

Kit did some stretching of his back and arms and even his neck. When he had finished, he glanced over at Jake.

"You married?" Kit asked.

"Who wants to know?" responded Jake.

"Me. I want to know," snorted Kit.

"Of course," Jake said.

"What does your wife think about your illegal antler business?" asked Kit.

"What illegal antler business?" responded Jake calmly.

"So, you don't tell the little woman about stealing antlers in a national park?" asked Kit.

"I tell my wife everything she needs to know and nothing that she doesn't need to know," said Jake.

"That I can believe," said Kit sarcastically.

"How about you?" asked Jake.

"How about me what?" responded Kit.

"Are you married?" asked Jake.

"Nope. I sure ain't," said Kit.

"Ever been married?" Jake probed.

Kit looked over at Jake and saw the sly smile on his face. "Nope. I never been married and do not see it in my immediate future."

"So, you never found some lady who grabbed your fancy, or you never found one foolish enough to see you as husband material?" asked a now grinning Jake.

Kit thought about the question and then answered it. "There's been some interest in the market, but nothing that resulted in a solid offer," he responded.

"In other words, she said no," laughed Jake.

"Something like that," responded Kit tersely.

"A swing and a miss!" said Jake and then he laughed.

"How much further to the motel?" asked Kit, trying to change the subject.

"We're about a mile away," replied Jake. "Should be there in a couple of minutes."

"Can't wait," said Kit. He reached in his pocket and pulled out a business card. He handed it to Jake. "All my contact info is on there," he said. "Send me your address and I'll mail you a check."

"Not a problem," replied a smiling Jake who took the card and stuck it in his shirt pocket.

Sure enough, Kit could see a faded sign on the side of the road announcing Myrest Motel. An electric vacancy sign hung below it, but it was not lit.

"Pull in and wait for me," said Kit. "I'll make sure they've got rooms available and then come out and retrieve my cargo."

"Works for me," replied Jake. He pulled into the parking lot of the motel. The motel building was an old one-story L-shaped building that had seen better days. The paint was peeling, and the parking lot was gravel and mud. Probably more mud than gravel. Jake pulled up in front of the short end of the L-shaped building, and there was a sign by a door announcing office.

Kit exited the van and almost tripped when he took his first step. His legs were stiff, and he paused for a moment to get feeling back into them. Then he walked through the door and into the office.

An elderly white-haired lady in a wheelchair was behind a small counter in the tiny office. She looked up from a paperback she was reading when Kit stepped inside the office.

"Can I help you, mister?" she asked.

"I need two rooms for the night," said Kit, as he reached for his wallet.

"Can I see some I.D., sir," the lady asked politely.

Kit handed her his driver's license and a credit card. She took them and ran the card and glanced at the driver's license.

"Can I have the license of your vehicle?" she asked.

"I have no vehicle," replied Kit. "My two friends and I had our vehicle break down, and we got a ride to your motel. The vehicle is being towed and should be fixed by tomorrow."

"Oh, dear," said the women. "I'm so sorry to hear that. You just can't depend on anything these days it seems."

She ran the card and gave Kit a receipt. Then she handed him two keys on plastic stubs showing the room numbers. "You and your friends have rooms 6 and 7. Each room has a queen-sized bed. If you need any additional towels, just come back here to the office. Thanks for staying with us," she said.

Kit nodded and headed out the door. He noted the office window facing the parking lot was high, above the elderly lady's line of sight from the wheelchair. He reached the van, opened the back, and had Roberto and Gonzalez get out along with their packs. Then Kit banged on the side of the van, and Jake drove off the lot and back onto the highway. In seconds he was out of sight.

Kit took room 6 and gave the key to room 7 to Roberto. "Gonzalez is your prisoner so he's now your problem until your friends show up. If you need me to help with anything, knock on my door." Kit looked at his watch. "I'll order pizzas and soft drinks. When they arrive, I'll call your room and we can eat in my room," he said.

"Fine," responded Roberto and he grabbed Gonzalez by the arm and led him to room 6. He used the key to open the door and pulled Gonzalez inside and shut the door.

Kit entered his room and tossed his pack on the floor. He got on his phone, found a pizza place nearby that delivered and made his order. Then he showered, changed into a clean shirt, socks, and underwear and pulled on his old jeans.

Twenty minutes later there was a knock at the door, and Kit opened the door to the pizza delivery gal. He paid the bill, added a tip and called Roberto on the phone. Almost immediately Roberto and Gonzalez arrived at his door.

Both men smelled the hot pizza and their mouths started watering. Kit grabbed Roberto by the arm. "Did you call and let them know where we are?" he asked.

"I did," replied Roberto and he wrested free of Kit's grip and headed for the pizza boxes. The three men wolfed down pizza and drank soft drinks. Eating overrode any conversation and when they had finished, Roberto and his prisoner left for their room and Kit locked the door and braced a chair against the doorknob. Then he flopped down on the bed, fully clothed, and was soon fast asleep.

Chapter Thirty-Two

Kit slept hard. He awoke once in the middle of the night to go to the bathroom. Too much Coke, he thought. When he awoke next, it was almost nine in the morning. Kit took a quick shower, shaved, and put on the shirt he had worn the night before as well as the jeans he had worn since this adventure had begun.

He walked to the motel office where he had seen a coffee service when he had checked in. Sure enough, there was fresh coffee. He grabbed a paper cup, filled it, added sugar, and powdered creamer. He stirred the cup, tasted it, and then made his way back to his room.

Once inside, he checked his phone for messages and sipped his hot coffee. He had some junk messages and some spam, but nothing urgent or important until he got to almost the bottom of the list of emails. The next to oldest email was from Swifty. Swifty never sent emails.

"Got call from that old geezer O.J. Pratt. Said you might be in trouble and need help. Where the hell are you and what the hell is going on?"

Kit chuckled to himself. For someone who prided himself on using few words, it was obvious Swifty was royally pissed at him. Kit thought for a minute and then sent an email in response.

"Long story. At Myrest Motel in Coram, Montana. Where you?"

"Swifty likes things short and sweet, and this is his kind of message," thought Kit to himself.

Kit finished his coffee and sat in the old chair by the bed. He turned on the television and watched the local news. The search in the park for Gonzalez was still the lead story. According to a spokesperson for the sheriff's office, law enforcement forces were closing in on the escaped convict. When a reporter asked for details, the sheriff's spokesperson did a remarkable tap dance and ended up providing no details whatsoever.

"Honesty is dead, especially in the media," thought Kit. He found an old movie and settled in his chair to wait for Roberto to get a call. After an hour and a half, the movie ended. Kit got up from the chair and decided to check on Roberto and his prisoner.

He knocked on the room door and Roberto opened the door just a bit so he could peer out at who was knocking. When he saw it was Kit, he opened the door and let him in.

"Hear anything from your people?" asked Kit.

"Yes," said Roberto. "They should arrive in the early afternoon. They told me to be ready to move quickly."

"How's Gonzalez doing?" asked Kit.

Roberto almost sneered at the mention of Gonzalez's name. "He's still breathing," said Roberto. "I made him sleep on the floor with his right hand cuffed to the leg of the bed. Close enough to keep track of and far enough away to keep him from getting any funny ideas," said Roberto.

Kit walked over and examined Gonzalez. The man was dirty, smelled bad, and was in a foul mood. He sneered at Kit, but wisely held his tongue. From the bruises on his face, Kit was sure Roberto had smacked him around a bit when he had been unruly during their stay in the motel room.

Satisfied Gonzalez was still alive and kicking, Kit got to his feet and faced Roberto. "Since we're going to be here for a while, I'll head to the office and see what I can find as a source for lunch that delivers. Do you have any preferences?" he asked Roberto.

"Mexican, if that's possible in a gringo town," replied Roberto.

"If there isn't any real Mexican food available, something like Taco Bell all right with you?" Kit asked.

"Close enough," responded Roberto.

Kit left the room and heard Roberto lock the door behind him. Then he made his way to the motel office. The old woman was on duty and Kit asked her about take-out food available. He learned he had been correct about real Mexican food, but she told him for a delivery fee he could get food from a few fast-food places, including Taco Bell. He got Taco Bell up on his phone and ordered enough food for half a dozen men. He included his credit card with his order and got an email that the food would be delivered within one hour. Satisfied, he went back to his room after helping himself to another cup of coffee.

Kit was reading the current stock market report on his phone when there was a knock at his door. He opened it a crack and saw the delivery girl. She handed him two large sacks and he gave her a five-dollar tip. He sat the food on the bed and went next door to let Roberto know lunch had arrived.

Kit barely got back in his room before Roberto arrived with Gonzalez in tow. The three men sat on the bed and the one chair in the room and attacked the sacks of food. For a period of almost fifteen minutes there was no conversation in the motel room. The only noises were of rustling paper and loud chewing sounds.

Kit put down the empty enchilada wrapper and wiped his mouth with a paper napkin. He took a drink of Coke and then looked over at Roberto. The young Mexican had a mouthful of burrito, so Kit waited until Roberto had demolished the food.

"Heard any more news from your people?" asked Kit.

Roberto grabbed a napkin and wiped his mouth before answering. Then he took a long drink of Coke. "Yes, yes I have," he replied.

"And?" asked Kit.

Roberto took another swig of Coke and then he responded. "They expect to be here by 2:30. We're to be packed and ready to leave immediately. Gonzalez is to be restrained both hand and foot."

"So, this is adios?" said Kit.

"No, no it is not," said Roberto.

"What do you mean?" asked a surprised Kit. "This was our deal. I guided you to Gonzalez, helped you capture him, and then guided you safely out of the park. My job is finished."

"I only know what I was told," said Roberto. "They said you were to accompany us along with Gonzalez."

Kit was not pleased with this change in plans. Roberto grabbed another wrapped burrito and began greedily devouring it. Kit sat back in the chair and pulled out his phone.

He checked his emails, and there was one from Swifty.

"Hang tight. The cavalry is coming."

"What the hell did that mean?" thought Kit.

He looked at the time on his phone. It was 1:45 P.M. Forty-five minutes wasn't a hell of a long time, but he knew it would creep along because he had no control or plan in place.

"Where the hell is Swifty?" Kit thought.

Chapter Thirty-Three

By 2:15 Roberto and Gonzalez had finished stuffing themselves with Taco Bell's finest and had returned to their room to pack. Kit packed his things back in his backpack. He extracted the small pistol and after checking to make sure it was loaded, he stuck it in his back pocket and waited in his old chair.

Kit wanted to see this thing through, and he planned to keep his word on finding and delivering Gonzalez to the cartel, because he wanted to part company with them on even terms. No harm, no foul. He didn't plan on ever dealing with them again. He didn't like this change in plans by people he didn't know and didn't trust any more than he trusted the federal government.

2:30 came and went and no cartel car appeared in the motel parking lot. Kit got to his feet and exited his room. He knocked on Roberto's room door, and it was opened quickly by Roberto.

"It's after the time you said they would be here," said Kit. "What's going on?"

"I got a text about five minutes ago," replied a worried looking Roberto. "They said they're running late and should be here by 3:00."

Kit looked exasperated, which he was. "Let me know if you get another text," he said.

"I will," replied Roberto.

Kit left the room and went back to the office for a cup of coffee. He nodded to the elderly lady and grabbed a cup of coffee from the dispenser. Then he returned to his room.

Kit checked his phone again. No email. No text. Nothing. "Technology was great except when it wasn't," he thought.

He texted Swifty again. "Where the hell are you? Running out of time," he texted.

Kit sat in his chair and watched as the small clock on the bedstand slowly moved toward three o'clock. About five minutes till three, he heard a vehicle pull into the motel lot. Kit got to his feet and moved to the window. Without exposing himself, he viewed the outside from an angle to the side of the window. A large black Chevrolet Suburban with Montana license plates pulled into the motel parking lot. The vehicle was clean as if it had just left a car wash. Kit was sure it was a rental.

Kit heard the door to Roberto's room open and then heard Roberto yell out a greeting in Spanish. He heard no response from the parking lot. Kit moved to the door and opened it a crack. He could see most of the lot and had a good view of the Suburban.

As Kit watched, Roberto walked toward the Suburban with his pack on and a downtrodden looking Gonzalez, hands and feet bound, shuffling closely behind. Kit stayed at the door.

The front doors of the Suburban opened, and two men got out. Neither man was familiar to Kit. Both men were young, in their twenties, and wore jeans and bright cowboy shirts with pearl snaps. Kit looked them over and smiled at the ostentatious cowboy boots on their feet. They certainly looked the part of cartel cowboys.

The four Mexicans met about five feet in front of the Suburban. Roberto extended his hand, but the two cartel cowboys ignored it. The taller cartel cowboy did all the talking. When he finished, Roberto pointed to the room Kit was in. The shorter cartel cowboy walked towards Kit's room.

Kit felt the small pistol in his back pocket. Then he checked the collapsible baton on his belt. Both weapons were ready and available in a hurry. He scanned the parking lot behind the three men and the Suburban. There was no sign of any help or rescue party. Even the traffic in front of the motel had dwindled too almost nothing.

Kit had a bad feeling in his stomach. The cartel cowboy was almost at his door.

Chapter Thirty-Four

Kit opened the door before the cartel cowboy knocked on it.

"Come in," said Kit as he stepped aside to give the cartel cowboy room to enter the small room.

The shorter cartel man entered the room slowly. He was nervous, and it was obvious. Nervous people made Kit nervous.

"Senor Andrews?" he asked.

"Yes, I'm Andrews," responded Kit.

"Please have a seat," said the cartel cowboy, pointed to the lone chair in the room. Then he stepped to the door and motioned for his partner to join them in Kit's room. In a matter of minutes, the small room was filled with Kit, the two cartel cowboys, Roberto and a now openly weeping Gonzalez.

In the room, Kit could see the two cartel cowboys had automatic pistols shoved in their belts, barely hidden by the colorful cowboy shirts hanging outside their jeans.

The taller of the two cartel cowboys spoke next. "Mr. Andrews, Mr. Cortez sends his greetings and extends his thanks for your part in finding and delivering Mr. Gonzalez to us," he said.

"Please tell Mr. Cortez thank you, for me," responded Kit.

"Mr. Cortez wishes you to accompany us to his residence," responded the taller cartel cowboy.

"I don't think so," said a now grim-faced Kit. "That wasn't part of our deal. I agreed to lead his team into the park and track and capture Mr. Gonzalez and then deliver him to Cortez's people. I have done that. My job with Mr. Cortez is complete."

"I'm afraid I must insist," said the taller carte cowboy with more than a hint of insolence and potential violence in his voice.

"Insist?" responded Kit.

"Si, I insist," replied the smart mouthed Mexican.

Kit could tell the young Mexican was enjoying his role of thug enforcer. Things were looking dim for the good guys. Kit paused as if thinking about what the Mexican had just said.

"Do I have a choice?" asked Kit.

"No, Mr. Andrews, you do not," said the cartel cowboy with obvious relish in his voice.

"Let me get my pack," said Kit.

He crossed to the bed and picked up his pack and slung it over his shoulder. The two-armed Mexicans directed Kit, Roberto, and Gonzalez out the door of the motel room and into the parking lot.

"Move to the truck," said the taller Mexican in a tone that was nowhere near friendly. It was an order, not a request.

Kit and the two other men began to walk toward the Suburban setting in the middle of the motel parking lot. They got about ten steps from the motel room door when a familiar voice rang out.

"Hands up, assholes!" commanded a loud voice that Kit knew as well as his own.

The two Mexicans stopped in mid-stride and whirled around to face the source of the voice. Both were reaching for the pistols in their belts.

"Touch them guns, and you'll get blown in half," snarled Swifty. "Your choice." He was baiting the two gunmen, and they knew it.

The two cartel cowboys had turned to face three men, all gringos. Two of the men were on either side of the motel room door. The other appeared from the direction of the motel office. Two of the gringos were tall, unpleasant looking men dressed all in black, including black cowboy hat and black masks that covered their faces. Even more unpleasant were the weapons they held. Each of the two men held a Benelli M-4 semi-automatic shotgun, the standard battlefield shotgun of the United States Marines. The third man was dressed in jeans and a plaid work shirt. He wore a cap with a logo on it and a black mask covered his face. He held an all-black Remington 870 riot gun with a short barrel.

Both the cartel cowboys literally turned pale. They froze in place.

"That's more like it," said Swifty. "Now slowly, with your left hands, pull out them pistols from your bellies and toss them over by my feet. You make any move I don't like, and I'll cut you in half. You savvy?"

Both cartel cowboys nodded their heads and followed Swifty's instructions. When they were disarmed, Swifty had them get down on their knees and stepped forward until he was about five feet from them. His black clad partner reached down and scooped up the pistols.

"I want you two yahoos to listen up, and I mean listen up well. I don't want no misunderstanding about what's going on here. Understand?" Swifty asked.

Both Mexicans nodded their heads they understood. Both men were obviously terrified. They had the look of men who in an instant went from being in control to being totally controlled by someone they feared.

Swifty then looked over at Kit. He motioned with his free hand for Kit to approach the two Mexicans.

"Good to see you again, Mr. Andrews," said a grinning Swifty. "Can you explain why these hombres forced you at gunpoint to leave your room and get in that there Suburban?"

Kit smiled. "They claim their boss wanted to see me in person, but that was not the deal I agreed to when I signed on to this job," said Kit.

"Well then, this sounds like some simple misunderstanding to me," said Swifty. He turned and looked both Mexicans in the eye. "You boys take these other two Mexicans with you to go see your boss. Then you explain to him that here in the good old U.S.A., we keep our word and this here deal between him and Mr. Andrews is complete. You savvy?"

Both Mexicans nodded their heads vigorously they understood.

"All right then," said Swifty. "You boys take your friends and get in that there Suburban and drive on outta here."

As the two frightened Mexicans got to their feet, Swifty added a warning.

"Just to be clear," said Swifty. "If anything unpleasant should happen to Mr. Andrews, we'll be comin' for you two and then we'll be comin' for this Mr. Cortez next."

Swifty then pointed to the waiting Suburban. "Adios," he said.

The four Mexicans wasted no time scrambling into the Suburban, and seconds later the big black SUV was careening out of the parking lot and onto the highway.

Chapter Thirty-Five

As soon as the Suburban was out of sight, Swifty and Kit embraced like the old friends they were. Then Kit hugged his half-brother, Billy. Finally, he hugged Jake McKusker. When he finished hugging everyone, Kit stepped back and looked directly at Swifty.

"Where in the hell have you been?" he yelled. "I thought I was in big trouble and suddenly I'm in the middle of a rerun of the gun fight at the O. K. Corral."

Swifty dropped the mask from his face as did Billy and Jake. Then he looked out at the vacant highway and smiled.

"Well, that's a long story. You know I ain't much for lots of talking. It makes my throat dry, so I got a suggestion," said a grinning Swifty.

"I'm all ears," replied a stoic looking Kit, even though he knew what was coming.

"I suggest we get the hell out of this place before someone sees all this nasty lookin' hardware and calls the cops. Let's get in my truck and find someplace quiet were they serve hot food and cold beer. Talkin' dries out my throat and I need to keep it watered," said Swifty.

"Lead the way," said a resigned Kit.

"Excellent choice," said Swifty and he led the way to an alley behind the motel where a big four door Ford half-ton pickup sat. The four men climbed in with Swifty in the driver's seat.

In less than fifteen minutes they had pulled into an old log tavern half hidden in the woods along the highway.

"This place looks good as any," announced Swifty and he led the way into the tavern. The tavern was old, but small and cozy. There was a big stone fireplace at the far end of the tavern. An old battered and scarred wooden bar ran along one wall with shelves of bottles above coolers of various vintages and ages. There was a small kitchen located behind part of the bar. A woman who had to be pushing seventy was tending bar, and there were only two patrons setting at the bar. Both were older men who looked to be well past retirement age. The bartender and the two men gave them a glance when they entered the tavern. Then they turned back to their conversation.

Swifty pointed to an old round table with five chairs. "Grab a seat, and I'll get a pitcher of beer," he said.

Kit, Billy, and Jake each grabbed a chair and took a seat. Swifty quickly returned with a tray containing a pitcher of beer and four frosty mugs. He set the tray down and handed out the mugs. Then he produced old plastic menus and passed them out.

"This joint is a bit short-handed, so I'll order lots of nachos and give them to the bartender," said Swifty. He returned to the bar where he somehow passed all that information to the lady. She nodded and took the menu's from Swifty. He returned to the table where the other three men had each poured a mug of beer and were busy wetting their whistles.

Kit waited until Swifty had poured himself a mug of beer and taken a long swig.

"Now that your throat is properly lubricated, just what the hell was going on and how did you, Billy, and Jake end up at the motel?" asked Kit.

"Oh no, you don't," said the previously silent Billy. "We'll tell you all that crap after you tell us just how you managed to get yourself in this ungodly mess."

Kit looked at his half-brother and sighed. "You're right," he said. "You deserve to know how I wound up in that two-bit motel with two Mexicans."

"Take another swig of beer to lubricate your throat and enlighten us," said Billy.

Kit grinned and took his half-brother's advice. He finished his beer and sat the mug down on the well scarred tabletop. "Fill up your mugs before I start. It's not a short story," Kit said.

The other three men smiled and took turns filling their mugs with beer. When they were finished, Kit began his story.

"It started at this high-class hotel I had just checked into after finishing an assignment. I was having a late breakfast when this well-heeled Hispanic man came up to my table and made himself at home. His name was Cortez, and he had a proposition for me to guide some of his people into the park and find this bad dude they wanted to get their hands on before the cops nailed him," said Kit.

"Why the hell would you agree to a deal like that?" asked a surprised Swifty.

"He had cartel boys in the place with guns on me," said Kit. "Agreeing to a strange deal seemed better than a bullet between the eyes."

All three men smiled and nodded their heads in agreement.

"So, we started this journey into the park. Me and these four Hispanic cartel guys. None of them had a clue about hiking in the mountains. They saw themselves as tough guys, but they were mostly kids with guns and some not in very good shape to be hiking in the mountains," said Kit. He related their pursuit of Gonzalez and they listened in silence, pausing for a sip of beer when the mood struck them.

Kit told them about running into an old friend on the trail when he encountered O. J. Pratt and his faithful burro. Kit mentioned he had run into O. J. several times before including when they were up in the Big Horn Mountains with Billy.

Kit went through his narrative, and they remained silent. Then he got to the part where they encountered the angry moose. When he related the moose's charge that tossed three cartel Mexicans off the cliff followed by the moose who was unable to stop his charge due to the loose rock under his hooves, there was a moment of shocked silence. Then the other three burst into laughter. Kit had to admit the story was pretty funny in telling it if you weren't one of the three Mexicans or the moose. He finished up with how they stumbled onto Jake and his role getting them safely out of the park.

Kit paused. He reached out and took a swig of beer. Then he looked at his three companions and said, "That's my story. Now I'd like to hear your side of what was going on."

Swifty cleared his throat and then took a sip of beer. "I got this phone call at the office from some cat named O. J. Pratt. At first, I wasn't sure who the hell he was. Then he mentioned our last meeting up in the mountains west of Sheridan. Once I remembered who he was, my ears perked up. He told me he ran into you on the trail up in Glacier National Park. I didn't catch on until he described where you were and who you were with. Now I know you're pretty capable for a tenderfoot, but you ain't no mountain guide. Sure, as hell not in Montana. So, I figured you were in trouble."

Swifty paused to take another sip of beer. "Damn, this is thirsty work."

"I'll get you another beer, Swifty. Keep talking," said Kit.

Swifty smiled and continued with his story. "I decided to get up to Montana in a hurry. O. J. had mentioned four Mexicans so I thought a little help might be a good idea.

Nobody in Kemmerer was around so I called old Billy up in Sheridan and filled him in. I packed what I thought I might need and chartered a two-engine plane out of Rock Springs. I flew from there to Sheridan and picked up Billy there. We rented a truck in Kalispel and while we were waiting for them to bring the truck out, I got a call from Jake forwarded from the office phone. I didn't know Jake from Adam, but he mentioned your name and so I called him," said Swifty.

Swifty paused for another swig of beer and then wiped his mouth off with his shirt sleeve. "Damn, that beer tastes good."

"All beer tastes good to you, Swifty," said Billy with a grin.

"I don't deny it none," said a grinning Swifty.

"Please continue with your story," said a slightly irritated Kit.

"Right, where the hell was I?" asked Swifty.

"You were calling Jake," said Kit.

"Yeah, right," said Swifty. "I called Jake and he told us what was goin' on and about dropping you and them two Mexicans off at that old motel. Me and Billy picked him up and drove to the motel. We staked it out early this morning. Them cartel boys took their own sweet time to show up. I was getting' tired and hungry. Pissed me off."

"How'd you know we were waiting for the cartel men to show up?" asked Kit.

"Jake told us," replied Swifty. "We set up a simple ambush to jump 'em when they came out of your room. Worked easy as pie. We knew from Jake that you wanted to finish your job with them on good terms. I ain't sure what the hell good terms are with cartel assholes, but I know how goofy you can get over crap like that. Anyway, we wanted to get them cartel boys and your two hikin' pals out of there and keep you safe."

"Which we did and here we are," chimed in Billy.

"Anything else?" asked Kit.

"Nope," said Swifty. "I'm hungry. Let's order some more food."

Jake decided to do something useful. He grabbed a battered plastic menu and went up to the bartender and order food for all of them. When he returned to the table, Swifty asked him, "what did you order?"

"Everything," replied a straight-faced Jake.

"I like this kid," said Swifty. "He's gonna fit in just fine."

Chapter Thirty-Six

Two hours later, after dropping Jake off at his van, Swifty pulled the truck into the parking lot at the Lodge at Whitefish Lake. As Kit exited the truck, he saw his truck parked in the lodge's lot. He checked his truck. The door was locked, and nothing looked disturbed. He returned to Swifty's truck and retrieved his pack. He shook hands with Swifty and Billy and promised to call them to meet for dinner.

"Be sure and get lots of rest," said Swifty. Then both he and Billy broke up in laughter. Swifty was still laughing when he drove off.

Kit had no idea what was so funny.0 He searched the pack and found his room pass.

Kit waved to Swifty and Billy as they drove out of the lodge parking lot. He made his way inside the lodge and within minutes he was in his room. It was just the way he had left it a few days before. He stripped off his clothes. His jeans were disgusting. They were torn and smelly. He decided to toss them. He went into the large bathroom and shaved and then took an exceptionally long, hot shower. He toweled off and walked over to the large bed. He slipped naked into it and was out like a light.

Kit woke up with a start as he felt a hand on his shoulder. Suddenly he was wide awake and ready to defend himself.

But, as his eyes adjusted to the daylight, the hand on his shoulder didn't belong to some Mexican cartel member. It belonged to someone familiar.

Standing next to the bed was Mustang Kelly. She was barefoot. She wore a short black robe that zipped down the front.

"Morning, Cowboy," she said softly.

"Morning," said Kit. "What the hell are you doing here?"

"All in good time, Cowboy. I think it's time for a hot tub," she said.

"Hot tub?" asked Kit.

Mustang pointed to the two-person hot tub out on the balcony of the room. The top was off, and steam rose from the hot bubbling water.

Then she unzipped her short robe, and it quickly pooled at her feet. She turned and walked slowly to the sliding door leading to the balcony.

Kit followed.

THE END

Acknowledgements

Much of this story could be true. None of it is. The beauty of fiction is it can be whatever you want it to be. This story came to me during a visit to Montana to see Glacier National Park. It's a great trip, and I recommend it to anyone who loves the West and the outdoors.

Ideas for a story just sort of invade my head when I least expect it. Once I actually had two ideas for a book at the same time. Usually, I'm lucky to come up with one. In this story, I wanted to have Kit in an unfamiliar situation with no friendly faces in sight. Then I wanted to have him use his experience and his wits to figure out how to solve his problem.

I brought back an old character and introduced a new one. I asked my old friend O. J. Pratt's permission to use his name again, and he graciously consented. Then I asked Jake McKusker, a friend and a fellow hunter, to use his name as I created a new character and he also agreed. Thanks again to both of them.

Back when I was in high school in Galva, Illinois, my principal noted I had extremely terrible handwriting, and he privately advised my mother I needed to take typing. I never said no to my mother. I and one other senior boy took typing in a class of sophomore girls. I disliked it, but

I learned how to type. I bought a portable Smith-Corona manual typewriter for college and then when computers arrived, my typing skills were easily adapted to a computer keyboard.

Even so, I make mistakes. I owe a great deal to my helpers. Chief among them is my wonderful wife Nancy, who proofreads all my drafts and makes plot change suggestions. In addition to Nancy, I have a small group of loyal friends who read all my drafts and send back corrections, possible revisions, thoughts, and ideas. I pay close attention to everything they say. They are a tremendous asset. They include Mary Marlin, Longmont, Colorado, a close family friend; Marcia McHaffie, Boulder, Colorado, a neighbor; Craig Morrison, Bethel, Connecticut, a college classmate and fraternity brother; and my oldest son, Steve Tibaldo, Athens, Alabama, a civilian employee of the U. S. Army. None of my books would have been possible without their help.

I am also happy to hear from readers about what they liked and didn't like in my books. I encourage you to let me know what you thought of this book by contacting me at **rwcallis@aol.com**. If you have a good idea for a book, pass it on and I'll see what I can do.

I write because I enjoy writing. I enjoy creating a story about something in a place both historic and real, and then letting my imagination take over. I get a sense of satisfaction when people read my books and enjoy them. Thank you for being one of my readers. Kit and Swifty exist only in my imagination. When I sit down at my computer, they come to life. What could be more fun than that?

Robert W. Callis

BOOKS BY ROBERT W. CALLIS

Kit Andrews Series

Other Books

Printed in the United States
by Baker & Taylor Publisher Services